EDDIE RED
UNDERCOVER

DON'T MISS EDDIE'S FIRST ADVENTURE IN ...

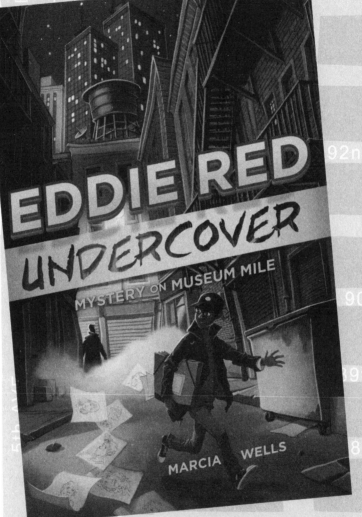

"Eddie is a smart, likeable narrator. . . . A sure pleaser for Cam Jansen grads or anyone fond of knotty, lightweight capers solved with brainpower."
—*Kirkus Reviews*

"Eddie Red is bound to be a series that will appeal to fans of fast-paced mysteries."
—*School Library Journal*

"Debuting author Wells creates engaging characters, teen and adult, and the friendship between Eddie and Jonah is well-drawn. A strong start to a promising new series, and as Eddie would say, it's über-cool."
—*Booklist*

A Spring 2014 Kids' Indie Next Pick

EDDIE RED
UNDERCOVER
MYSTERY IN MAYAN MEXICO

MARCIA WELLS

ILLUSTRATED BY MARCOS CALO

HOUGHTON MIFFLIN HARCOURT
BOSTON   NEW YORK

www.hmhco.com

The text of this book is set in Adobe Garamond Pro.

Library of Congress Cataloging-in-Publication Data
Wells, Marcia.
Mystery in Mayan Mexico / by Marcia Wells ; illustrated by Marcos Calo.
p. cm. — (Eddie Red undercover)
Summary: "On vacation in Mexico, Eddie Red and his best friend
Jonah must once again rely on Eddie's talent for drawing and his
photographic memory to uncover clues to catch a crook when Eddie's father is
falsely accused of a crime." — Provided by publisher.
ISBN 978-0-544-30206-8
[1. Drawing—Fiction. 2. Memory—Fiction. 3. Art thefts—Fiction.
4. Ghosts—Fiction. 5. Mayas—Antiquities—Fiction. 6. Indians of
Mexico—Fiction. 7. Mexico—Fiction. 8. Mystery and detective stories.]
I. Calo, Marcos, illustrator. II. Title.
PZ7.W4663Mxm 2015
[Fic]—dc23
2014016094
[Fic]—dc23
2014013599

Manufactured in the United States of America
DOC 10 9 8 7 6 5 4 3 2 1
4500520717

To Riley and Allison,
for teaching me the meaning of the word *silly*

The town and island depicted in this book are fictitious.
The Mayan gods and ancient treasure are not.

DEAD MEAT ... AGAIN

I'm back.

Or should I say, *He vuelto*. Because I'm in Mexico. In prison. Next to a guy named Raúl with weird body hair and a bad habit of picking his teeth with a large knife.

Okay the Raúl part's a lie. But I *am* in a Mexican jail, or at least in a small holding cell in the police station. The cops handcuffed me and fingerprinted me, and now I'm waiting behind bars to call my parents. That spells *J-A-I-L* where I come from.

And I do have a cellmate. Jonah "El Frijol" Schwartz (*frijol* means "bean," as in "Mexican jumping bean," as in "Jonah is a complete spaz"). He hit his head kind of hard and is currently asleep on a bench, snoring with a *honk-honk-weee* sound. A few minutes ago I shook him to make sure he wasn't slipping into a coma — and to get him to cool it with the *honk-honk-weee* thing. He blinked at me and muttered something, so I guess he's all right.

Don't get me wrong. Jonah's my best friend, and of course I care if he's hurt. But if you had just spent the past two weeks in Mexico with El Frijol, you'd be glad he's unconscious too.

I hear footsteps. A guard approaches, the same stocky older man who clomps by every ten minutes or so, refusing to acknowledge my existence. *"¿Teléfono?"* I ask for the hundredth time. He whistles a zippy tune and looks the other way.

I *have* to call my parents. It's almost midnight, and they must be seriously freaking out. I stand up to get the guard's attention, and wince. Cuts cover every inch of my body. My clothes are stained with blood— mine and Jonah's—along with a fair amount of Jonah's barf. I smell *awesome*.

"Oye, muchacho. Teléfono," another guard grunts in a thick accent. He's wearing a blue starched shirt with a star on each shoulder, and I think I heard the other guard call him Capitán, so I'm pretty sure he's the man in charge. I'm also pretty sure he's the guy who cuffed me back on top of the Mayan pyramid, but everything was a little blurry with the driving rain

and wind in my eyes. It's a miracle I didn't lose my glasses.

He slides the bars open, the metal rattling loudly in its frame. Jonah groans, rolls over, and bumps his forehead against the cement wall. The snoring starts up again.

I follow the captain over to his desk, doing my best not to limp or get water on the floor and failing on both counts. He scowls at the puddle I leave behind. The Darth Vader costume I'm wearing — don't ask — is dripping water like crazy.

"*¿Hotel?*" he says.

"El Hotel Cisneros," I reply.

He nods and dials, then hands me the phone.

In shaky Spanish, I tell the receptionist my parents' room number, then wait as the phone rings. And rings. My pulse pounds in my ears. What if they don't answer? What if they're out looking for us in this terrible hurricane? If anything happens to them, it will be all my fault.

"Hello? Er . . . *¿Hola?*" my father's deep voice answers.

"Hi, Dad." I try to sound upbeat, but I'm barely holding it together because every inch of my body is throbbing and he's going to kill me and I just want to go home.

There's a strange static sound, followed by muffled words and high-pitched noises like a small engine trying to turn over. I brace myself.

"Edmund?" my mom says. "Are you there? Are you okay?"

"Hi, Mom. I'm fine. I—"

"Where are you?" she demands. "Is Jonah with you? He'd better be."

I swallow hard. "Yeah, he's here. We're with the police. As their guests. Kind of."

"The *WHAT?!*"

I cringe and hold the phone away from my ear. I'm sure everyone on the island can hear her shriek. "We're coming to get you," she growls. "We'll catch a cab and be there in ten minutes."

"Uh . . . no." Here comes the bad part. "We're on the island. You know, La Isla del Niño?" The Island of the Boy, but they *really* should rename it the Island of the Dead Boy, at least in my case. "So you need to take a boat." I pick at the cast on my wrist, the wet plaster leaving chunks of white mush on the floor. Should I mention that I mangled the cast and need a new one?

Silence.

"Mom?" Oh, no, she's keeled over in shock. Can moms have heart attacks at age forty-two? "Mom, are you there? We did it. We solved the case, and . . ." My voice dies in my throat. I should have learned my lesson back in New York. Parents do *not* like it when you call them from jail, even if you caught the bad guy.

"We'll be there as soon as we can." Her tone could melt steel. I can practically smell the anger through the airwaves. Sort of a cross between burnt rubber and sulfur. "You're in a lot of trouble," she adds.

"I know," I whisper. "See you soon." With a sigh, I hang up.

"*¿La mamá?*" the captain asks.

"*Sí,*" I reply. "*La mamá.*" La mamá is very mad-o. Edmund is dead meat-o. Not that I blame her for being upset. This is the second time in two months I've landed myself in police custody. Just wait until she sees that I'm covered in blood. Again.

I try to stand, but the captain motions for me to stay put while he pulls out a few first-aid supplies, along with a Spanish-English dictionary. After putting on his reading glasses and flipping through the pages, he points to my wrist and says, "Break?"

I nod. "Fractured," I mumble. "Long story."

"*Cuidado,*" he replies. "We be . . . careful." With gentle fingers, he rolls up the black polyester sleeves of the Darth costume to examine the various scrapes and cuts I have on my arm. He dumps a clear liquid on my wounds.

"Ow!" I yelp as it bubbles and burns. The sharp smell of hydrogen peroxide slices the air. *How about some nice soothing antibiotic cream?* I want to say.

When he tries to apply more of the liquid acid to my skin, I shake my head politely and pull my arm away. I don't care if my cuts get infected. That's the least of my worries at the moment.

He shrugs and stands up, gesturing for me to return to the cell where El Frijol is now crumpled in a heap on the concrete floor. The captain hurries past me and kneels beside Jonah. He lifts Jonah's eyelids and shines a penlight in his pupils. "Okay," he says after a few seconds. I guess that ends the thorough medical examination.

"Okay," I agree, for lack of something else to say. I want to ask him if the evil Juan Guzmán is in jail or in the hospital, and if our friend Julia got the message that we're safe, and if the gold we found truly *was* the stolen bank treasure. But I can't. There's no way we can get through that conversation without a translator. So instead I step over Jonah's body and head for the now-empty bench. The cell door clanks shut behind me.

I lie down on the hard wooden surface. It's actually pretty comfortable. I squint at the bright fluorescent lights flickering overhead. I need to stay awake. I need to formulate a plan for surviving my parents' wrath. I need to review every single detail of the past two weeks in my photographic memory, because there will be *a lot* of police reports to fill out tomorrow.

It's going to be a long night.

Chapter 1

MR. Q

TWO WEEKS AGO

Arrival in San Pablo del Niño, Mexico

"Ancient treasure," Jonah says, staring at a glass display case in the middle of the hotel lobby. Inside the case rests a green jade mask inlaid with pieces of gold, c. *450 B.C.* stamped on a plaque below it. "This place is beyond awesome," he adds in a breathless voice.

We just arrived after a long flight from New York. Jonah's right. This hotel is über-awesome. Hot July sun spills in through the tall windows, the smells of pineapple and flowers float in the air, and an enormous pool complex shimmers just beyond the main doors, complete with water slides and a lazy river. It's better than the pictures in the brochure. It's . . . paradise.

I smile, my first real smile in weeks. I've been grounded this summer, stuck inside my apartment in New York City. No TV, no Internet, no phone calls, no Jonah. Just hours of quiet time to "contemplate and reflect on my poor decisions." Namely, ones that involved me, the police, a group of bad guys known as the Picasso Gang, and an alleyway shootout. And while I do this "reflecting," I also need to prove that I'm responsible and trustworthy, so I clean and dust every surface in the apartment at least once a day. Oh, and I scrub toilets.

It's as fun as it sounds.

But today I am a free man. Free for the next two weeks.

Still smiling, I look around the lobby at the tourists. There's an interesting mix of people. We've only been here five minutes and already I've heard Russian, German, Italian, and Spanish. *Click.* I take pictures of their faces in my photographic memory, good faces to draw when I'm bored and trapped at home after this trip is over. *Click.* A teenage girl with pink hair and six-inch silver hoop earrings. *Click.* A sunburned man in a Red Sox cap, jabbering on his cell phone in Russian.

"Do you think it's real gold?" Jonah whispers. He's

still staring at the display case, keeping his voice low, as if he's worried the mask is going to come to life if he speaks too loudly. The mask *is* sort of creepy with its sneering mouth and two empty eyeholes.

"Probably," I say. I shift to the left to get a closer look, when a man with a mustache and an ugly red Hawaiian shirt bumps into me. He's mesmerized by the display, pressing his nose to the glass and leaving streaks, practically shoving me aside with his elbow to get a better view. And I thought New York had pushy tourists.

Squawk! A birdcall echoes across the lobby. Two exotic blue birds are perched in a huge silver cage in the corner. One is cleaning its iridescent feathers with a curved yellow beak, while the other flaps its wings and complains.

"Let's go get changed." I pull Jonah toward the front desk, where my parents are checking us in. I'm hot and sticky from traveling and need to swim *immediately.*

"You're in room 407," Mom says when I come up beside her. She holds out two keycards. "We're in room 413. I wanted adjoining rooms, but they insist there are none available. You both better be on your best behavior." She glares at us like we've already set a wastebasket on fire (which happened once in fourth grade and *NEVER* again). "I know you're independent city kids, but you're only eleven, and—"

"I'm twelve, Mrs. L," Jonah says while looping an arm around my neck and pulling me in for a noogie. "I'll handle this young whippersnapper."

I shove him off and hiss, "*Not* helping our case, Jonah."

Mom presses her lips into a tight line. Jonah was definitely not her first choice for this trip. Five days ago she got a call from her boss, Larry, asking her to attend a real estate convention in Mexico. Larry was supposed to come with his family, but an emergency came up. So he asked Mom to take his place and gave her a free trip for four to reward her for all her hard work. We're only a family of three and wasting money makes Mom break out in a nervous rash, so she called *everyone* in her address book to fill the fourth spot, from my uncle Jay to the secretary in her office to our batty old neighbor Rita, who smells like cabbage. Rita, Mom? But it was the same answer every time: no one could leave on such short notice. No one but Jonah, that is.

"They'll be fine," Dad reassures her while shooting

me a look. His mustache gives a *Don't make me regret this* twitch.

"Great, see you at dinner," I say as I snatch the keycards from her, grab my suitcase, and shove Jonah along. A quick elevator ride up, a jog down a hallway, and we're in.

The room is small but nice—two beds, a TV built into a chest of drawers, and a round table with two chairs tucked in the corner, all the same white wood decorated with floral patterns as in the lobby. I yank back the curtains to reveal a postcard-perfect view of a white beach and rolling ocean waves. There's a green island off in the distance.

Grinning, Jonah and I high-five. "I call top drawer," I say. I open my suitcase, dump the contents into the drawer, fish out my bathing suit, and slam the drawer shut. I scurry into the small bathroom to change, then grab my goggles and flippers. "Ready?"

"No. Give me five minutes." Jonah has opened his suitcase and removed two huge Ziplocs filled with bottles and tubes. I sigh and sit down on the bed. We're going to be here at least a half hour.

"Just so you know," he says, "I will be posing as a Man of Culture on this trip." He air-quotes the words. "There are mysteries everywhere in Mexico, and we're going to solve one. Take a look at this." He grabs his enormous backpack off the floor and drops it onto my lap.

I gasp as two hundred pounds of bricks land on my thighs. "What do you have in here? You're going to get scoliosis lugging this much weight around." I sound like my grandmother. But I don't want a lecture on whatever crazy plans he has right now. I want to go dive for stuff with my new snorkeling gear.

"Keep yourself occupied," he says. "You need to study up."

Study on vacation? I open the zipper and peek inside. Cautiously. You never know what you're going to get with Jonah Schwartz. I expect to pull out some kind of weird Man of Culture disguise, complete with a fedora, a bushy mustache, and maybe some wire-rimmed glasses, but instead all I find are hardcover books from the library. Modern ghost mysteries, a history book called *The Aztecs and Mayans: Ancient Civilizations of Mexico,* and an especially enormous volume entitled *The Aztec Gods and You: A Practical Application.*

"Planning some human sacrifices?" I ask. That *is* what the Aztecs are famous for, after all.

"Page forty-one," he says over his shoulder as he marches into the bathroom with an armload of toiletries. "Meet Quetzalcoatl, the god who's going to help us."

I crack open the book. I might as well do something useful, since Jonah won't leave until everything is in its place, each bottle and brush sitting exactly two inches from the edge of the shelf. Obsessive-compulsive disorder — it's part of his charm.

Page forty-one has a cool picture of a fanged creature wearing feathers and holding a twisting snake, the words *Quetzalcoatl: Aztec God of Intelligence* at the bottom of the page.

I scratch my arm. A hot arm in desperate need of refreshing pool water. "Quetzal . . . how do you say this again?"

He comes back into the room and starts to carefully fold his clothes and place them in the bottom drawer of the dresser. "I think it's Ket-sal-co-at-el. I'm calling him Mr. Q for short. He's going to help us on our quest."

"And what quest is that?" I ask, warily eyeballing the picture of the snake.

Jonah never stops moving. He pulls out clothes and books and more clothes, arranges them in their proper spots, then pulls out more. Apparently he can fit a freaky amount of stuff in his suitcase. "I figure we solved a major police case back in New York," he says. "So why not tackle Mexico? There are tons of unsolved crimes down here. They need our expertise."

He's serious. He actually thinks we're going to throw ourselves into another police investigation. "No way." I slam the Aztec book shut. "I'm retired."

He folds his arms across his chest. "Look, you got to be Eddie Red, and all I got was a stupid sinus infection. I want in on the next adventure. All the way this time."

Last winter, the NYPD secretly hired me because of my photographic memory and my ability to draw near-perfect pictures. They gave me the code name Eddie Red (long story) and used me as a human camera to hunt down a gang of art thieves. Then Jonah and I decided to solve the case ourselves. It was going really well until he got sick and had to stay in bed while I ended up duct-taped to a drainpipe in an alley (an even longer story). Not something I want to repeat any time soon. Plus, if I get in trouble again I'll be grounded until I'm sixty.

"It wasn't an *adventure*," I say through clenched teeth. "I almost got shot!"

He holds his hands up in surrender. "All I'm saying is, let's keep our options open. Forget the crime thing. We'll try a ghost mystery. There are tons of them down here with all the ancient spirits floating around."

"Fine." A ridiculous idea, but I'll humor him. He'll be distracted soon enough with the water slides and the lazy river. "Can we go to the pools now?"

"Not yet. Just one more thing to take care of." He pulls out a gift bag with *Hotel Cisneros* printed on it. Opening the bag, he shakes out a small brown statue with a key chain attached to its head. It looks like a short man with a Buddha tummy and a stick in his hand.

I wrinkle my nose. "What's *that?*"

He beams at me. "Meet Mr. Q." He makes the little statue dance in the air. "See the snake he's holding? Cool, right? I asked the lady in the gift shop if they had any Quetzalcoatl guys kicking around, and they did. Our luck has already begun!"

"You bought something at the gift shop?" I swear I haven't left his side since New York.

"You were in the bathroom." He makes Mr. Q do a swan dive in the air, followed by a *whoosh* sound like a jet taking off.

"How'd you pay for it?" I demand. "Did your parents give you a credit card?" May Quetzalcoatl help us all if this kid has no spending limit.

He snorts. "As if. I used cash. You know, pesos?" He gives me a *Duh, everybody has pesos* look. "I exchanged my money in New York before we left."

Resting the statue on top of the TV, he examines it while popping a piece of gum into his mouth. His face brightens. "Will you draw him?"

"What, now?"

"Yeah. In case I lose him. A security measure." He shoots me a *Pleeeaase* look.

"Fine." I grab my art pad and charcoal pencil. This is nothing new. I've been sketching his toys for him since kindergarten, including homemade Lego zombies, a moss-covered pet rock, and a weird ball of lint he named Fuzz Face. "But you have to promise we'll go swimming in the next ten minutes." I squint and start to sketch the bizarre Buddha-man.

"Yes, sir." He salutes me, then gets back to studying Mr. Q. "Now I have to figure out what to feed him. A sacrifice." He snaps his fingers and digs into

MR. Q

the suitcase one last time, conjuring up a huge jar of peanut butter and a plastic knife. "Sharing my peanut butter is a *major* sacrifice." He scoops out a glob and smears it on Mr. Q's stomach. "He's going to help us on our mission to find a ghost, maybe dig up some buried Aztec treasure."

I've had enough of this. "First of all," I splutter, "gross. We're going to get bugs in here. Like, huge man-eating cockroaches. And second, we are *not* on a mission. We're on vacation. I'm grounded, remember? You better not cause trouble, Jonah. My mother's nervous enough as it is. We're on vacation," I repeat.

Pop, chomp, chomp, pop. He smacks his bubble gum and offers me a toothy grin.

"Whatever you say."

Chapter 2

LUCK

DAY 2

This morning, we're rolling onto a ferry with my parents, and I do mean *rolling*. I just ate my body weight in pancakes at the best breakfast buffet ever—huevos rancheros, breakfast burritos, waffles, chorizo, bacon . . . mmm, bacon—even though I was still full from yesterday's steak-dinner extravaganza. The last thing I want to do right now is ride on a boat in choppy waves, but this is Mom's only day with us all week, and we promised her we'd do some sightseeing.

A woman greets us as we board the ship. She's in a sharp purple suit, wearing a name tag and a pleasant smile. "Welcome, Familia Lonnrot," she says. "I'm Marita, the hotel's tour guide." Her English is perfect, without the slightest accent. She turns to me and Jonah. "My daughter came for today's island visit when she heard there were kids her own age." She points through the semi-crowded boat to a girl sitting in the back, then motions for us to continue down the aisle. "Please join her. She's a much better guide than I am." She winks.

I catch Jonah's eye and he shrugs. Hanging out with a girl we don't know might be painful, but so will listening to my father's dorky comments about the nutritional makeup of salt water and the science behind why coconuts float.

I turn and head between rows of plastic benches as the boat rumbles to life. It's the kind of boat that has a roof but no solid sides, just railings that allow the ocean air to whip around us as the waves rock us back and forth. I've almost reached the last row when the blob of pancakes in my stomach lurches. I stop to steady myself and Jonah knocks into me from behind with an *"Oof!"* I stumble forward and almost land in the girl's lap.

Mortified, I step back as the girl stands up, her big hazel eyes growing wider by the second. No doubt she's alarmed at the bumbling American circus that's just arrived. She's quite pretty, with tanned skin, almond-shaped eyes, and high cheekbones, her features similar to the drawings of the native people in Jonah's *Ancient Civilizations of Mexico* book.

"Hello," she says, pulling her long black braid over her shoulder. "I'm Julia." She pronounces her name *Hoo-lia,* with a soft accent on the first part. A nice name.

"I'm Edmund," I say. I don't make a move to shake her hand because she might think that's weird, plus I'm sweating like a beast. It's only ten in the morning but already ninety-five degrees out, the sun a blazing fireball that promises to melt the flesh off my bones.

She nods and fiddles with her braid, then glances at Jonah. He stares back at her without a sound. No movement, no twitches, *nada.* I clear my throat and nudge his arm. Still staring.

Uh-oh.

It's as if he's brain-dead: glazed blue eyes, mouth hanging open. I give him a sharp yet subtle jab in the ribs with my thumb.

"Hi!" he says in a chipper voice as if nothing Extremely Socially Awkward has just happened. "I'm Jonah." As he speaks he pushes me into the bench so that I'm by the railing. He steps in next, doing a little hop move like a jolly leprechaun, his curly red hair wild from the humidity. Sitting down, he motions for Julia to join him on the other side. She giggles.

I roll my eyes and move over to make room. At least the breeze is cool on my sweaty skin as we start to pick up speed, the vast ocean stretching out before us.

"I'll be your tour guide," Julia says over the hum of the engine. "Today we're taking a short trip to La Isla del Niño. It's just up ahead."

"Boy Island," Jonah translates for me, as if he and I aren't in the same Spanish class back home. "Sounds cool." He thrums his fingers on the seat, then he pats the pocket of his backpack, where Mr. Q is resting, and flashes me a grin as if to say, *See? We've met a cute local girl who's going to help us find buried treasure. Our luck's really taking off.*

The boat picks up speed, bouncing on the waves. My stomach does a somersault. *Don't get sick, don't get sick,* I think over and over.

"Are you okay?" Jonah asks. "You're kinda pale green, which is really saying something."

I groan and clutch my stomach. "I feel pale green." A gag rolls in my throat. This is it: I'm going to puke on him and completely ruin his first-ever cute-girl encounter.

Julia leans toward me with a concerned expression. "Look out at the horizon," she says. "It will help."

I nod and stare at the island ahead, a cool stone pyramid coming into focus as we get closer. I hope I won't be too sick to climb it.

"So tell me about the ghosts on the island," Jonah says to Julia, his voice loud over the noise of the engine.

"Um . . ." Julia hesitates, as if she's not understanding his words. I want to reassure her that her English is fine and that Jonah is obsessed with finding an unsolved ancient mystery, but I keep my comments to myself. She shakes her head. "No ghosts. But there's a very old temple and a museum that sells souvenirs. Also a police"—she waves her hand like she's searching for a vocab word—"headquarters. With a small marina. To catch the drug traffic on the boats?" Her explanation ends in a question, as if she's unsure of her language abilities.

"Your English is really good," I say. It's terrific, actually, with just a slight rolling accent.

She blushes. "Thank you. We practice at home.

My mother is American. She moved here with my grandfather when she was ten. He was an archaeologist, just like his father before him."

"What about Aztec treasure?" Jonah says. "Any unsolved mysteries?"

She frowns. "We're in the *Mayan* Riviera." She gestures to the coast behind us, to the white beaches and swaying palm trees. "The east. This is where the Mayans lived, thousands of years ago. The Aztecs lived in the west." Her frown deepens with disapproval. There's a possibility that she thinks we're ignorant American tourists. Which I guess we are.

Jonah presses on, unfazed. "Did the Mayans have buried treasure?"

Whatever Julia's about to say gets cut off by a roar of the engine. The boat jerks and shudders to a stop. We're here. Through the crowd of excited tourists, I see Dad up front in his yellow sun hat, a glob of white sunscreen on his nose. He gives me a big grin and a wave. I smile weakly.

"Please stay in your seats, everyone." Marita's voice is tinny over the loudspeaker. "We'll let you know when it's safe to disembark."

"Edmund, look!" Jonah leans over me and points over the side of the boat.

I look at where he's pointing. The pyramid looms large above the beach, surrounded by a thick green forest. Its jagged stones are gray and tall, with a set of rock stairs running up the middle. Some sort of ancient temple with crumbing walls sits at the top.

The pyramid is ginormous and impressive, but that's not what Jonah's talking about. He's pointing to the left of the center staircase, where red liquid is oozing down the stones. Paint? Blood? A strange chill sweeps the hairs on my neck.

"Start taking pictures with that brain of yours," Jonah whispers. "This smells like a mystery in need of our services."

I stare at the creepy scene, wishing my eyesight were sharper. Are those letters in the middle of all the chaotic red? Some kind of graffiti is on the temple wall, written in blue. It's hard to tell because we're at least a hundred feet away. And what looks like white flower petals tumble in the breeze, sticking to the messy puddles. I really hope it's red paint. Otherwise, something very large and very bloody died up there.

Click. I snap mental pictures. More writing. *Click.* A pile of crumbled rocks. *Click.* Once the images are in my mind, I can recall them at any time and analyze the details as if I'm looking at a photo. Although right now the photo is too far away, too fuzzy. We need to get closer.

I turn to ask Julia what's going on, but she's gone. I spot her up in the front of the boat talking to her mom.

"I see an aleph," Jonah says, pointing to a rocky outcrop on the beach, far away from the temple. The boulders are draped in seaweed and shells from the outgoing tide.

"A what?"

"An aleph. It's a Hebrew letter."

I squint, but all I see are some green squiggles. "You see Hebrew everywhere," I say. "Remember the pizza incident?" Jonah's been taking a ton of extra Hebrew classes for his bar mitzvah next year. Last November he thought he saw a gimel (the Hebrew letter *G*) made out of red pepper on his pizza. He saved the piece of pizza in his locker, where it grew mold over winter break and turned a hideous shade of green. The school had to fumigate the entire east wing because of the smell.

"I can't help it if there are divine messages in my food," he says. *Tap-tappity-tap-tap.* He thrums his fingers on the seat in front of ours. The balding, sunburned man sitting in front of us turns to glare at him. Jonah stops tapping and sits on his hands. "You'd think you'd *want* your co-detective to be good with details," he adds.

I'm about to remind him yet again that I'm fried on the whole Eddie-Red-detective thing when the boat engine churns to life behind us. We're moving . . . backwards?

"Sorry, folks," Marita announces over the noise. "They're calling us back to the hotel. A storm's coming."

A storm? But I thought it was supposed to be sunny all week. People start pointing out the other side of the boat. I lean around Jonah and see huge black clouds gathering on the horizon. Where the heck did those come from?

The water is much choppier on the return trip. *Don't throw up, don't throw up,* I chant in my head. A strong wind picks up, slapping large waves against the side of the boat and spraying my face. My glasses get splattered, but I'm too queasy to clean them.

"Why isn't Mr. Q helping us?" Jonah says. He rubs the little statue, then gives it a shake. "Maybe he's putting us through a test."

"Maybe he's allergic to peanut butter," I mutter. I close my eyes. *Breathe . . . just breathe.*

Jonah mumbles something beside me. More shaking and a *pop* sound. I open my eyes in time to see him dip Mr. Q's feet in a small container of strawberry jam that he swiped from this morning's buffet.

When we arrive at the hotel, the beach is oddly deserted. No one's playing in the surf or kayaking or building sand castles. There's a red warning flag up, signaling it's too dangerous to swim. The few people out there are packing up their towels and heading into the hotel. *Plink, plink.* Fat raindrops splatter on the metal roof of the boat.

My parents get off the boat first and wait for us at the end of the dock. Even on dry land, my legs are wobbly and my stomach sloshes. We trudge up to the hotel in irritated silence while thunder rumbles overhead. More and more darkness sweeps the sky. We're supposed to go on a snorkeling trip this afternoon. *No fair!* I want to yell at the clouds.

"I don't want to be stuck inside all day," Jonah whines.

Mom flicks a nervous glance at him over her shoulder, no doubt worried about the same thing. Dad yanks open the big glass doors to the lobby, and we step inside.

What the . . . ?

We've entered a war zone. Policemen are everywhere, some searching bags by the wall while others attempt to direct people away from the front desk. Still more are winding yellow police tape around the jade mask's display case in the center of the room. But the glass case is empty, its small door hanging wide open. The hotel staff is running around, barking orders in Spanish too fast to understand, and to top it all off, there are signs up everywhere in Spanish and English, indicating that the pools are closed for the day because of the storm. Things cannot possibly get worse.

"Señor Lonnrot?" A gruff-looking policeman approaches my father, glaring at him with dark, beady eyes. When my father nods, the man holds out his hand and gestures impatiently. "Come with me," he says in a thick accent. "You are wanted for questioning."

Things just got worse.

Chapter 3

LOCKDOWN

———

"I still think we should call someone," Mom says, pacing the floor of my parents' hotel room. A difficult task since there are three bodies and a king-sized bed in the way. Jonah and I are parked in the twin chairs by the window, while Dad is sitting on the edge of the bed, rubbing the back of his neck.

"I can't believe they questioned you without a lawyer present," she says. Pace, pace, pace. "And they fingerprinted you! Is that even legal? I feel so helpless. Should we call the U.S. embassy? Where is it, Mexico City? Maybe I should call my office. Larry travels a lot. He might know what to do." She plops down beside my father.

"It's fine," he reassures her. "It was just a formality. They questioned a few other guests as well. Anyone seen touching the display this morning."

She frowns. "You touched the display?"

He stares down at his fingers, still stained from being fingerprinted. "You know I have an inquisitive mind."

"But you didn't touch the mask, did you?" she says.

"Of course not. The case was locked. I, uh . . . checked."

Mom's frown deepens to a scowl. "What else did they say?"

He scratches his mustache the way he does when he's gearing up for a long story. We may be here a while. I open the art pad that I grabbed from my room and start to sketch with a pencil. I am a police sketch artist, after all. Maybe I can provide a few leads for the cops. *Anything* to get them to leave my father alone.

"Someone stole the jade mask from the lobby," Dad begins. "A bellboy told me all about it. It was there one second, gone the next. There are no security cameras, and the guy working the reception desk claims he was checking on a delivery when it happened. Quite a coincidence, I'd say."

As my father talks, I flip through pictures in my mind of the last eighteen hours. Our arrival, the pool, the restaurant, the faces of the different guests . . . anyone suspicious. Three people stand out: the man with the mustache who bumped me yesterday by the mask display, a woman in the lobby who was shifting her hands nervously in and out of her purse, and an older guy at breakfast who had a gold ring on every finger and made a joke in a thick New Jersey accent about having to rob the hotel in order to afford this vacation.

My pencil flies across the page. I loosen my shoulder to make sweeping lines: an oval for the head, small curving place-markers for the eyes, nose, and mouth. Mustache man had a medium-length nose, short brown hair, youngish face, tanned skin. Completely ordinary except for his eyes. Eyes that were an unusual murky gray.

"What if they decide to arrest you because of your prints?" Mom says when Dad finally finishes. Her voice is muffled since her face is now buried in her hands. "Have you *heard* about Mexican prisons? Maybe we should go home."

Dad smiles. "Let's not overreact. We all know I didn't steal anything, so there's nothing to worry about. You need to focus on the convention. I'll call the embassy if it makes you feel better. But it will be fine." My father is the most upbeat person in the world.

FIRST SUSPECTS

I move on to the woman's portrait. Shifty, narrowed eyes, a round face, thin lips. My arm is tense and shaking from drawing so fast, but no one's paying attention to my spazzy movements.

"It's supposed to rain the next few days," Dad adds. "I'm going to relax here with the boys, do some reading. Maybe I'll even start working on that mystery novel I've always wanted to write."

My hand freezes and I glance up. Mom and I share a confused look. "A novel?" Mom asks.

He nods and flashes us a huge grin. My father, the very large man who thinks sweater vests are a good idea, the über-nerd who spends hours on the Internet researching ways to grow plants without soil. *He* is going to write a mystery novel?

"I've already worked out the plot," he says. "A mystery set in ancient Mayan times. Did you know that the Mayan city of Chichén Itzá was abandoned back in the fourteen hundreds? The people just left and went to live in the jungle. No one knows why. The city's only two hours from here. We'll go this week."

Mom snuggles against his broad shoulder, telling him what a great idea it is and how proud she is of him. At least she's not freaking out anymore. And Dad's novel has given me an idea . . .

"Sounds great," I say. "We'll be good and let you work, I promise." Writing will occupy him so Jonah and I can snoop around and try to get some answers. We'll solve this case by dinner tomorrow and enjoy the rest of the vacation in peace.

Dad looks at his watch. "No more moping around. We'll go to the art museum in town this afternoon. They have a terrific exhibit of Mexican painters. Works by Diego Rivera, Frida Kahlo . . . some really impressive stuff." He pats his stomach. "It's almost lunchtime. Let's meet in the dining room in twenty minutes."

"Okay. We'll be in the arcade until then." I stand to leave, Jonah right behind me. He's been eerily quiet the last half hour, sitting and rubbing Mr. Q's stomach, working the peanut butter and jelly into a gooey paste.

Out in the hallway, Jonah's limbs jolt to life as if he's been electrocuted. "What's the plan? Tell me you have a plan!"

I walk to the elevator and stab at the down button with my thumb. "We need to scout the area, maybe talk to the hotel staff."

Jonah grins. The door opens and he does a happy little shimmy into the elevator. "I need a cool code name," he announces. "Maybe Mr. Q Junior. Or Super Q." He frowns down at the little statue in his hand, then pulls out a safety pin from his pocket and pokes the tip of his finger. Blood bubbles to the surface.

"What are you doing?" I ask in alarm. This is very un-Jonah-like behavior. Usually he hates germs and dirt and stains of any kind.

"Upping the sacrifice. We need major help." He dabs blood on Mr. Q's belly. "I know what you're thinking. Usually messy stuff freaks me out. But this"—he gestures up and down his body—"is a carefully crafted calm. Mr. Q is giving me strength. Are you in?" He holds out the pin for me.

I shake my head. "No thanks." I'm about to ask how blood and peanut butter are truly going to help our police work, when the elevator doors open and we step out into the lobby. Showtime.

Quickly I survey the area. "I'll talk to that guy." I gesture with my chin to the cop who questioned my father. He's alone in the far corner, putting papers in a briefcase. "You walk the perimeter."

Jonah's eyes flit around the room. His back and shoulders go rigid as he shifts into military mode. "Agreed," he says. "Meet back at base in five minutes.

Failure is not an option, soldier." And with that, he stuffs his hands in his pockets and walks away.

I clutch my art pad with sweaty fingers and approach the policeman. I wish I could tell him about me being Eddie Red and how I worked for the NYPD, but I can't. I had to sign a million documents swearing I'd never reveal my role. I just hope that when this guy sees my pictures, he'll realize I'm a professional.

"Sir?" I say in a voice I wish weren't quite so shaky. He doesn't respond, just keeps shuffling through papers, his head bent low. His slicked-back hair is perfectly combed, his mustache neat and trimmed. Everything about him is crisp and organized.

I try again. "Um, señor?" What do I call him? He has no name tag on his sky-blue shirt, no badge that indicates his rank. A star on each shoulder, but what does that mean? Detective? Inspector?

Shuffle, shuffle, shuffle. "*¿Qué?*" he finally grunts, not looking up.

Okay, he gets irritated easily. I can handle this. I have *plenty* of experience with grumpy policemen, namely Detective Bovano, Detective Bovano, and . . . Detective Bovano. I paste on a charming smile. "Sir, I know you've had a bit of trouble here in the lobby. And I wanted to let you know that I have a photographic memory and I'm good at drawing. I'm sort of like a human surveillance camera." I open my art pad. He's still staring down at his briefcase, but at least he stopped flipping through his papers. I take it as a sign to continue. "I have a couple of pictures I drew of some suspicious—"

"You tourists are all the same," he interrupts. Now he's looking at me, really glaring at me with eyes as hard and cold as his clipped movements. "Always interfering, thinking you run the show. You think because you have money, you have answers."

I jerk the art pad back in surprise. "I'm not wealthy," I say. Not even close.

He raises an eyebrow. "So you need money, do you? Are you desperate enough to steal?" His accusatory gaze rakes over me and all kinds of alarm bells go off in my head. This guy obviously hates tourists, and probably hates Americans. So where does that leave my father?

"Go back to your room, *gringo,*" he says. "Go get your father a good lawyer." He snaps his briefcase shut and leaves without another glance in my direction.

WHAT? The alarm bells have cranked up to fire-engine shrieks in my skull. Why does my father need a lawyer? Dad may be a huge geek who stared at the jade mask for twenty minutes this morning, but he is *not* a thief. And how does the cop know who my dad is? I mean, we look a lot alike with our dark skin and thick glasses, but we're not the *only* black family in the hotel. Plus I'm skinny and short, while my father is a hulking house of a man.

I spin on my heel and storm over to the elevator. Jonah's nowhere in sight. I find him back in the room, sitting on his bed and sketching a map of what looks like the lobby. SpongeBob laughs loudly on the television (his cartoon voice is just as annoying in Spanish as it is in English). Jonah mutes the program and throws the remote on the mattress. "What happened?" he says, his eyes widening at the anger on my face.

I grab Mr. Q from his perch on the television, along with the safety pin from the table. "We have a big problem," I say. I prick my finger and smear blood across the statue's peanut-butter-and-jelly stomach. "I'm in."

Chapter 4

MI CASA, SU CASA

DAY 3

"I made you some *dulce de leche*," Julia says as she hangs up our wet raincoats. Twenty-four hours later, and it still hasn't stopped raining. "It's a kind of Mexican caramel." She beckons us forward. "We'll eat in my father's office, no?"

"Sounds great," Jonah says. "Thanks."

We took a cab to Julia's house this morning for two big reasons. First, it turns out that her great-grandfather was the archaeologist who discovered the jade mask. Jonah found that out last night when he was prowling around the lobby in search of bottled water. The mask belongs to her family and was on loan at the hotel.

The second and more important reason is that her father's the chief of police. The chief of police! Which makes Julia our number one lead in the investigation.

She told Jonah we could go through her father's papers. Finally some good luck.

We follow her down a long hall lined with colorful red and orange tapestries. This is it—free rein in a police office! I'll sift through files and recent faxes while Jonah hacks into the computer, both of us looking for answers to the only question that really matters: what kind of evidence do they have against my father?

The office is tiny and quiet, with a minuscule filing cabinet and no electronics. Disappointment washes over me. Where's the police database? The list of evidence? *You've had less to work with before*, I remind myself. *You can do this*. I'll just have to use my police smarts and Jonah's über-brilliant brain to figure this out.

A picture on the wall snags my attention. It's a black and white photo of a group of policemen, including the mean cop from the hotel. "This guy is a jerk," I say, pointing to the man with the slick hair and the angry scowl. "I think he wants to send my father to jail just for being a tourist."

Julia looks to where I'm pointing. "That's Capitán Ruiz. He hates kids, tourists . . ." She frowns. "He hates everybody."

"Is he racist?" My new fear: maybe the captain is after my father because of the color of his skin.

She shakes her head. "I don't think so. I've never heard him speak that way. He is an ambitious man. Years ago my father was promoted to *comandante*. Ruiz was very angry. He wanted the job. He still does."

Does he want the job badly enough to send the wrong man to jail? I think of how my dad looked this morning, typing the first pages of his novel. His shoulders seemed more slumped than usual. Is he upset about the police?

Shoving my worries aside, I sit down on a small couch and unzip Jonah's backpack. I find a bottle of iodine, a jackknife, three lighters, a plastic gun—how did he bring all this junk on the plane, let alone get it past customs?—and a small jar of peanut butter. Not to mention a mountain of books.

Finally I locate my detective supplies and open my sketchpad, which is already partially filled with pictures I drew yesterday. What I thought were strong leads last night seem flimsy and weak today. The thief could be anyone: a tourist, a delivery person, a random person walking by . . . Anyone in the town of San Pablo del Niño. And that anyone is probably long gone by now.

Jonah's standing over by a shelf filled with plaques and trophies, his fingers twitching as if he really, *really* wants to poke at something until it breaks. He's quiet, and I realize he's letting me take the lead. I guess I *do* have experience with police interviews, although usually I'm the one being questioned.

I can do this. I can lead my own police interrogation. But where to begin? I flip past a drawing I did from memory of the stolen mask. That seems like a good place to start. "Why don't we talk about the mask," I say to Julia. "Jonah said it belongs to your family?"

Julia's face falls. "Yes," she says. "We were going to sell it so my father can retire. He's older and has heart problems. And now . . . now . . ." Her eyes fill with tears. Oh, I really hope she doesn't cry.

In a panicked move, I pat her on the back with awkward thumps. "The police will find it, don't worry," I say. "Do you have any idea who might have stolen it?"

She shakes her head, her big eyes growing sadder by the second. This line of questioning is only mak-

THE STOLEN MASK

ing her more upset. I switch tactics. "I need to know why they questioned my father. Do you have any reports about the mask? Something that might mention my dad's name?"

"No," she says. She sits down at the desk and clears her throat. "My father is away, helping my uncle in Oaxaca. He will get the reports when he returns." She offers me a plate loaded with thick chunks of dulce de leche, as if sugar's going to make everything better. "He is supposed to be here tonight."

"Oh," I say. If there are no reports, what are we doing here? I stuff a piece of candy in my mouth before I say anything I'll regret.

"Let's look at local criminals," Jonah pipes up from the corner where he's fiddling with a potted cactus. He comes over and sits down beside me on the small couch. "We'll see if this crime fits a pattern. It could be someone with a police record, right?"

"Okay." Julia pulls open the filing cabinet. It rattles and squeaks as if it's a hundred years old, which it probably is, judging by the rust on its gray paint. She pulls out a thick file and hands it over. "The only real crimes we have around here are from a gang called Las Plumas."

Jonah flips open the file. A stack of pictures spills onto his lap, snapshots of statues and staircases covered in red paint, just like the scene we saw at the temple yesterday.

"Whoa!" he says. "Is that *blood?*"

"Yes," she replies. "Bloody scenes are their specialty. Don't get too excited," she adds quickly, as if she can sense that Jonah is about to launch into a huge story about zombies and chainsaw massacres. "It is only cow's blood. The Plumas steal blood from the . . . *matadero.* The place where the cows are killed for meat. Then they dump it on local monuments."

"They must have been the ones who decorated the temple yesterday," Jonah says. He snorts. "Doesn't *plumas* mean 'feathers'? Not exactly a tough gang name."

"They are local kids playing pranks. They spray paint political messages on walls. And they have tattoos on their wrists of a black feather." She turns back to the filing cabinet to dig through more folders.

I add Las Plumas to my list of suspects, although I doubt a group of teen punks could pull off a heist of Mayan treasure. I also add the guy who was working the front desk during the robbery. According to my dad's information, he was the only employee on duty who had access to the key that opens the glass case. Very suspicious.

Local suspects:
1. Las Plumas—"The Feathers Gang"
2. The lobby desk clerk

"There is only one other famous crime in our town," Julia says. She heaves out a battered brown folder stuffed with yellowing pages. "An unsolved mystery."

At the words *unsolved mystery,* Jonah sits at attention. I grab the huge folder from Julia's extended hands and open the file, only to discover a dense pile of newspaper articles. I understand two words: *robo,* which means "robbery," and *banco,* which means "bank." My sixth-grade Spanish class didn't exactly prepare me for Mexican crime-scene investigation. I glance up at Julia for more explanation.

"This is the one case the police never solved." Julia scoots her chair over so that she's right next to Jonah. His face lights up like he just won the lottery. "About thirty years ago, a man named Pablo Valero stole an ancient Mayan necklace from a local collector. While the police swarmed the area, he went after his real target, the National Bank."

"Like chess," Jonah says. "Distract your opponent, then attack where they don't expect it."

She blinks at him in surprise. "That's exactly what my father said." Smiling, she offers Jonah a small cup. "Milk?"

"Sure. Thanks." He grabs the bottle of iodine from his backpack and sprinkles a few drops in the glass, turning the white liquid a muddy brown. He's scared to get Montezuma's revenge, the stomach bug tourists sometimes catch from drinking the water. Apparently iodine kills bacteria, but all Jonah's doing is grossing everyone out and making his food taste horribly bitter. Last night he made me try iodine on some orange slices. I had to brush my teeth twice to get rid of the awful taste.

Shuffling through the stack of papers, I pick up another article, entitled *El oro está con mi niño*. This one I can actually read. " 'The gold is with my son'?"

Julia nods. "That's what Pablo claimed. After he robbed the bank, he tried to escape by boat, but he was caught. When the police captured him, the bank gold was gone. Buried somewhere. He said the gold was with his son. He died two days later of a heart attack."

"And what about the son?" Jonah says.

Julia shakes her head. "There were no birth records, nothing that said he had a son." She shrugs. "That is all the crime we have here. San Pablo del Niño is a quiet town."

So far we've got less than nothing. I sift through more pages while thinking of a polite yet quick way to return to the hotel. A picture of the bank robber leaps out at me, a mug shot with the name *Pablo Valero* printed beneath. I squint at his grainy face. "Impossible," I murmur.

Thumbing through the pages of my art pad, I flip to the picture I drew of the mustached guy in the red Hawaiian shirt, the guy who was breathing all over the glass the day before the mask was stolen. I hold it up next to the newspaper photo. Same nose, same angle of cheek bone, same rounded chin. Is it the same person? The man in the lobby had gray eyes. It's hard to tell from the newspaper article if the bank robber's eyes are dark or light.

"Holy Quetzalcoatl," Jonah breathes. "Is that . . . ?"

"Yeah," I say. "I think it is." I shift my sketchpad

TOURIST
GUY

PABLO
VALERO

so Julia can see it. "I drew this picture of a man I saw in the lobby," I explain, "the day before the mask was stolen. Could it be the bank robber's son?"

"Maybe." She bites her lip. "A strange coincidence. We should show my father this."

Maybe that's all it is, a coincidence. "Do you have any other pictures of the thief?" I ask. I've flipped through all the newspaper articles in the folder, but all I've found is the slightly blurry mug shot. I need more to go on. I start to sketch his face based on the photo, hoping that the clearer lines of my pencil will help us figure this out.

Julia rolls her chair back to the desk and opens the filing cabinet again. "I don't think so, but I'll look."

"Maybe this Pablo Valero guy never died," Jonah says. "And he had really good plastic surgery." His twitching leg picks up speed, rattling the papers on my lap.

"Not likely," I say. "The man in the lobby was young. His skin wasn't stretched tight in that weird plastic way."

Jonah holds up a hand. "They can do amazing things with surgery these days, Edmund. Maybe he escaped with the bank gold but the government covered it up and faked his death. We have to investigate *all* possibilities." His eyes have taken on a wild conspiracy-theory gleam.

"Fine." I sigh and add the man to my list:

3. Mustached man who might be a bank robber's son. Or the bank robber himself with perfect plastic surgery.

Jonah chatters away about how cool it would be if this was an old unsolved mystery *and* a lost treasure mystery all wrapped into one. I'm barely listening, my mind whirring a million clicks per second. Blood and feathers, gangs and gold . . . This is impossible. I'm trying to solve a crime in a language I can barely speak, in a culture I don't understand, and with no police support or solid information.

Julia glances at me with a sad expression, as if she's thinking the same thing I am.

There is no way we can solve this.

Chapter 5

TOSSED

DAY 4

Rain, rain, and more rain. I've been sitting in the lobby all morning, watching every person who walks by. I've drawn twenty more faces, twenty more possible suspects. But who am I kidding? I've got nothing. Just a clerk, a gang, and a Ghostman. Jonah insists we call the tourist guy that since he looks exactly like the dead bank robber, Pablo Valero.

When we returned to the hotel yesterday, two policemen were dusting every inch of the lobby for fingerprints. What if they find my father's prints in a weird place? Knowing Dad, it's entirely possible. The cops also removed the glass case and pedestal from the center of the room, so now there's just a weird open space where the ancient mask once sat. The emptiness stares at me like a gaping eye, mocking me and my über-pathetic detective skills.

"Soldier Schwartz, reporting." Jonah plops down in a chair beside mine and hands me a stack of papers. "The desk clerk's name is Luis Gusto. By all accounts, he's kind of dumb. Shows up late for his shifts, keeps a sloppy workstation." He stretches and cracks his knuckles. "His uncle is a rumored drug lord. Not sure if that's important. We'll know more when I hack into the personnel files on the computer system."

Jonah's been interviewing the employees with Julia's help, pretending to do a report on Mexican hotels for a kids' magazine. Everyone knows and loves Julia — her mom's worked here forever — so it's been a pretty smooth operation so far.

I nod and look down at the papers he gave me. It's a list of the employees, their job descriptions and daily routines. The names are color coded in red, yellow, or green to indicate level of suspicion, based on the employee's schedule and proximity to the mask.

Jonah stands up. "I gotta go. Julia and I are playing chess in the employee break room while monitoring staff movements. You okay?"

"Sure. See you at lunch," I say. He leaves with a big wave in my direction. I glance down at my watch:

10:20 a.m. Two more hours of drawing faces and listening to the blue birds screech in their cage.

A flash of lightning lights up the room. I look up as the lobby doors fly open, and drop my pencil in surprise. In storms Captain Ruiz with three policemen following closely behind. Ruiz sees me, glares, then stomps over to the elevator, practically running over an elderly couple. He's the meanest man on the planet. I drew a picture of him yesterday in case it turns out he's the mastermind criminal and we need a recent image.

Wariness pricks the hairs on my neck as he disappears into the elevator. What's he up to? One minute ticks by. Two minutes tick by. I'm just about to pack up my sketching supplies and head to my parents' room when Dad walks off the elevator looking really upset. I jump out of my seat.

"Dad, what's—"

He holds up a big hand. "It's okay. The police have a warrant to search both of our rooms. They asked me to wait down here. It's okay," he repeats. He sits down on the nearest couch and offers me a strained smile.

"Okay?" I echo in disbelief. "It's not okay, Dad.

CAPTAIN RUIZ

What if—" I cut myself off. What if Ruiz is up there planting evidence? Julia says he wants the chief of police job. What if he stole the mask and is framing my dad, all so he can solve the case quickly and be the big hero? I slump into the seat beside my father.

He pats my shoulder. "We have nothing to hide. They won't find anything, and it will all blow over. I'll call a lawyer as soon as we get back into the room." He adjusts his thick glasses and looks down at my art pad. "What are you up to?"

"Drawing the birds." I flash him a picture of one of the birds, my cover-up sketch for parental probing situations like this.

"That's nice." He's in distracted-robot mode. Poor guy. He shakes his head as if clearing his thoughts. "We're still on vacation. Let's go to the arcade once the police leave. Blow off some steam and have fun. And don't forget, tonight's French night."

I know he's trying to cheer me up, but he's just making it worse. Every night the main dining room holds a theme dinner, such as seafood night, Mardi Gras, and casino night. Tonight is French night, when they'll have French food, music, and costumes. Guests are encouraged to dress for the occasion. Dad brought a purple beret from home, and that's all I'm going to say about that.

He clears his throat. "Look, I know we have an honesty rule, but let's not tell Mom about this, not yet. She has to focus on the convention. Larry promised her a promotion if she delivers down here. It will be a big increase in salary, and we need the money. We'll tell her back home." He sighs and adds, "Please don't tell Jonah, either."

Jonah . . . I forgot about Jonah. He's going to have a complete meltdown if they touch his stuff. Plus I really hope he doesn't have anything illegal up in the room. Is Mace legal in Mexico? He may have brought some nunchucks as well.

We sit in silence. Dad crosses his legs, uncrosses them, taps on one knee. He's wearing a yellow Hawaiian shirt, the buttons undone to reveal a green T-shirt with a lounging frog in sunglasses and the words *Stay Classy* printed at the bottom.

Time grinds to a halt. Fifteen minutes . . . twenty minutes. Dad picks at his nails while I draw and draw, the only thing that keeps me sane.

Thirty minutes . . . forty minutes . . .

Ruiz and his men step out of the elevator. My father leaps to his feet before I can blink. I don't think

I've ever seen him move so fast. I follow, hot on his heels to catch what Ruiz is saying:

"Your cooperation is noted," he says to Dad. "You will hear from us if we have further questions." Then he smiles a very evil smile. "You may need to call housekeeping." And with that, he leaves.

We watch him go. Well, *Dad* watches him go. I watch Dad, concerned for his mental state. His jaw is tense, and a muscle twitches beneath one of his eyes. I don't think he's breathing.

"We'll straighten the rooms," he suddenly announces. He holds out an arm to escort me to the elevator. "It will be like it never happened."

I nod, not trusting my voice.

This is the worst vacation ever.

Chapter 6

CHAAC

—

DAY 7

"Hey, *chico*." A man in a stained chef coat is standing in front of me, rubbing the ends of his bushy mustache. I'm sitting in the lobby for the fourth day in a row, drawing faces and glaring at the rain.

"*Ven conmigo,*" he says.

I look at him blankly, so he clarifies with a "Come with me" in a thick accent. He motions for me to follow him through a set of white doors labeled EMPLEADOS. "Employees Only." I hesitate. This has major potential to be a Stranger Danger moment. Follow a random person somewhere in a foreign country? Not a good plan. But I've seen Julia joking around with this guy, so I'm sure he's okay. Maybe he has information about what went down in the lobby.

"They call me Papi," he says over his shoulder as we

push through a set of swinging doors and into a huge kitchen. "I am head chef at Hotel Cisneros."

Sounds like an important position. So what does he want with me?

Papi's shirt and apron might be stained and rumpled, but his kitchen is sparkling clean. Every stainless steel surface shines: stoves, grills, countertops, blenders, knives . . . everything under the sun that cooks, cuts, or fries. Several men are standing in front of one of the counters, chopping mountains of vegetables and singing along with the radio. Seeing that there are at least five other people in the room and I'm probably not about to be abducted, I relax a little.

Papi brings me over to the far side by the refrigerators, where a few stools are lined up by a silver metal countertop. He motions for me to sit and places a plate of custard and cookies in front of me. "Please eat," he says. "I made you a special flan. And *pastelitos de boda*. Mexican wedding cookies."

The flan is a wobbly brownish-yellow custard that reminds me of boogers. The cookies are small balls covered in powdered sugar. I go with option number two.

"Thanks," I say. Why am I getting the royal treatment? I take a bite of cookie. It's good but über-sugary. "I'm Edmund," I say through a mouthful of crumbs. I rack my brain for polite conversation topics. "Your English is very good." *Now, why did you ask me back here and what do you know about the crime?*

He beams at the compliment, smiling so wide I can see the gold in his back teeth. Then he grows serious and runs a broad hand over his mustache. After glancing around the kitchen, he leans forward as if to tell me a secret. I stiffen and inch back without being too obvious.

"I see you do the"—he struggles a moment, searching for a word—"the art. The drawings." He motions to the pad in my hand. "You are good."

"Thanks." I shift uncomfortably on the hard stool. Where is he going with this?

He rolls up both sleeves of his white coat, revealing tattoos that cover each forearm. "These are my girls," he says proudly. "Marisol, María, Clara, Juanita, and little Isa. They are beautiful, no?"

"Uh . . . sure." I stare down at the faces on his skin. The tats were done when the girls were little, either babies or toddlers. Over the years, his flesh has obviously sagged a bit, and now the faces are kind of droopy. Tattooed faces always creep me out. They never look lifelike, and with weird shading around the mouth and cheeks, the faces always appear to have a faint beard. *Not* okay on a baby.

"You can draw us a family picture," he announces. "A special present for Marisol's wedding."

"Uh," I say again. This is getting weirder by the second.

He claps his hands. "I worked in Colorado. I know how this goes with you *gringos*. You want money?"

I shake my head. "No, I—"

"Good, because I don't got no money." He guffaws like it's the funniest joke ever, his big belly rolling up and down, side to side. It's kind of hypnotic. Still laughing, he dips a hand in his back pocket, producing a fat wallet stuffed to the max with papers. He fishes through it and yanks out a wad of pictures.

"Here," he says, shoving them into my hands. I struggle with the stack, trying not to drop any. His daughters are now in their late teens and early twenties, all with long black hair and wide smiles. Attractive in a jolly Papi kind of way.

Papi strokes his mustache with slow sweeps as if deep in thought. He speaks softly. "You do this for me, I do you a favor. Yes?"

"Oh. Um, okay." I tuck the photos in my art pad for lack of a better place. I guess I can do this for him. It won't take long. Plus having a favor from Papi might come in handy. The whole thing feels sort of Mexican gangster.

"*There* you are." Jonah's voice yanks me out of the mobster moment as he walks into the kitchen, Julia close behind him. If she's surprised to see me hanging out with Papi, she doesn't show it.

"We've been looking for you," Jonah says. "We have new information, and—" His words grind to a halt as he eyeballs the huge, shiny knives that hang from the racks on the walls.

I sit up straight. "Information? Is your dad back?" Julia's father hasn't returned from his trip. He was supposed to come home days ago, but the roads are flooded from the storm. He *has* to get back here. I need access to police reports, and he's my only hope.

She shakes her head. "He's still stuck. But I heard my mother talking to him on the phone. She was saying that—"

"They suspect someone with a mustache!" Jonah interrupts. I glance over at the other cooks, but they're still busy chopping vegetables, oblivious to our discussion. Papi is pulling some bags of shredded cheese from the refrigerator.

Julia scowls. *"Bobo,"* she snaps (I can only imagine what *that* means). *"I* was telling the story." She glares at him a second longer, then opens a cupboard and roots through it. I like Julia. Behind her sweet smile and huge hazel eyes is a no-nonsense girl, a girl who will put Jonah in his place.

"Sorry," Jonah says, grinning and not looking sorry in the slightest. He parks himself on the stool beside mine. He's been in a great mood, completely unaware that our room was searched three days ago. The room actually wasn't in bad shape, but I still spent an hour making sure his clothes were neatly folded and his toiletries placed precisely two inches from the edge of the bathroom counter.

I mentally digest the new information. The police suspect a man with a mustache . . . Everyone down here has a mustache. Papi, my dad, the evil Captain Ruiz, our Ghostman suspect, *everyone.* It's like a huge mustache convention exploded in the hotel lobby.

"Why are you in the kitchen?" Jonah says.

I tell him about Papi's family and the pictures he wants me to draw. As I speak, I watch Papi chop onions on a nearby counter. His knife flies over the surface like lightning, onion bits springing up into the air. He's lethal with that thing.

Jonah's fingers tap on the counter like drumsticks. "A favor from a local adult. Excellent." He pokes at the flan on my plate, then pops two cookies into his mouth.

"Ready?" Julia says to Jonah. She sets down a carton of milk, a piece of bread, and a small green pepper.

He swallows the wad of cookie. "Yes," he mutters, his bony shoulders sagging.

I raise an eyebrow. "What's all this?"

It's Julia's turn to grin. "I beat him in chess. Now he has to try a pepper. A jalapeño."

No one has beaten Jonah at chess. *Ever.* As she turns her back to us to grab a glass off the shelf and pour him a cup of milk, I whisper, "Did you let her win?"

"Are you kidding me?" He shakes his head. "I don't want to eat a hot pepper. Plus there's the germ thing. We're only supposed to eat vegetables that are peeled."

Julia places the food in front of him. "Remember,

milk and bread are better than water," she says. "And don't eat the seeds. I'll go first." She nibbles a dainty bite of pepper. "You see? Not so bad. Then I have a little bread, and the heat fades." She breaks off a small square of bread and eats it.

Jonah's eyes dart from the partially eaten pepper to Julia, back to the pepper, back to Julia, a small smile curling at the corner of his mouth. I know what he's thinking: Does it count as a kiss if your lips touch where the girl's lips were touching a few seconds ago?

He shrugs and picks up the pepper. "Sure. Easy." He takes a bite, a bigger one than Julia did as if to prove his manhood. He chews and chews and chews. Sweat beads on his forehead, and his eyes start to water. "No problem," he rasps.

"Bread, Jonah," I say in alarm as his lungs squeak and his face turns so red that his freckles stick out like pale stars.

He holds up a shaky hand. "Gluck unngh. Rolp. Unnngh."

"Jonah?" Julia says, her palm resting on his convulsing back.

He stumbles off the stool and pushes blindly past me, practically throwing his body into the sink. All fear of the tap water is forgotten as he shoves his face under the faucet and gulps down buckets. Then he lifts his soggy red face from the sink and beams at us. "I'm okay," he announces in a gurgly voice. Grabbing a hand towel, he wipes off his mouth, then blows his nose. I'm sure he's just violated about a thousand health codes, but Papi doesn't seem to mind. In fact, he's laughing so hard it looks like his stomach's going to jiggle off.

Julia shakes her head in amusement. "I'll get you some peanut butter for your bread," she says. She heads over to the other side of the kitchen, where industrial-sized jars of ketchup and mustard line the shelves. I wonder if Jonah's considered dropping Mr. Q into one of those. Probably.

Jonah shuffles back to his stool, still wiping his face. He pulls a bottle of iodine out of his pocket and puts a few drops on his tongue. "Just in case," he says. I stifle a gag.

Papi's laughter dies down and he gets back to chopping vegetables. *"¡Ay, El Frijol!"* he says. *"¡Muy famoso este Frijol!"*

Jonah and I share a confused look.

"Sí, señor," Papi booms. "Jonah 'El Frijol.' And his

friend, Edmund 'El Rojito.'" He gestures to my red baseball cap with the knife in his hand. I know *rojo* is "red," so *Rojito* must mean "Little Red." I think I like Eddie Red better.

Jonah frowns at Papi's words. "What does *free-hole* mean?" he says to Julia when she returns with a butter knife and a small bowl of peanut butter. As he speaks, he shovels another cookie into his mouth.

She smiles. "It means 'bean,' or 'jumping bean.' Because you move around a lot." She illustrates Jonah's patented leg twitches. She stops and puts her hand on his arm. "He is only joking."

Jonah doesn't look upset in the slightest. As he stares at the hand-on-arm contact, his cheeks turn the same color as his hair. He giggles. Julia giggles in response and doesn't take her hand away. Somebody shoot me now.

Papi says something to Julia in Spanish. She nods and follows him over to yet another huge refrigerator, where they continue talking at a thousand words per second while loading up two plates with pastries. Hanging out with Papi in the kitchen clearly has some major advantages.

On the counter to the left of us is a metal pan

with a huge side of raw beef surrounded by blood. Jonah dips Mr. Q in the tray when the chef isn't looking.

"Gross!" I hiss at him. "You won't drink milk because of germs, but you'll splash around in cow's blood?"

"I'm not *licking* the blood, am I?" He shakes off the excess liquid, leaving Mr. Q stained a brownish red. "Nothing's working. Things are just going from bad to worse. Maybe he's lonely. I saw a bunch of Mayan gods in the gift shop. Maybe I'll get Acan, the god of wine. He'd be a fun buddy to have. Or maybe Mr. Q needs a girlfriend . . . There's Awilix, the goddess of the night. I've been studying the Mayan books your dad brought. There are a lot of cool Mayan gods out there."

He's going to buy another statue? I'm not sure how I feel about this.

He holds up Mr. Q. "Do you know anything about this Aztec god?" he says to Julia, who's just walked over with a truckload of chocolate croissants. "I keep giving him sacrifices for good luck since he's the god of intelligence, and things keep getting worse."

"I don't know." Julia makes a face. "He smells strange. Is that blood?"

Papi waddles over and plucks Mr. Q from Jonah's sticky grip. "This is Chaac," he says, as if that explains everything.

"No, it's Ket-sal-co-at-el," Jonah says, very proud of his careful pronunciation. "He's holding a snake, see?" He points to the small snake in Mr. Q's stone grip.

"*No, señor,*" Papi says. "*Lo tengo en casa.* I have it at home. He is Chaac, rain god of the Mayans. My ancestors. He is holding a . . . what do you call it . . . *hacha.*" He looks at Julia to translate.

"An ax," she says.

"*Sí,* an ax." Papi nods in a whole-body jiggle. "The Mayans say Chaac hits the clouds with his ax, makes rain and . . . *relámpagos.*" Again he looks at Julia.

"Lightning," she says.

Rain and lightning. Rain and lightning. All this terrible weather, this terrible luck, is *JONAH'S FAULT?*

"Oh," Jonah says quietly. Papi hands him the statue and returns to his work, chuckling to himself about *"gringos locos."*

"A rain god?" I spit out. "You've been making sacrifices to a *rain god?*" I glare at Jonah, who at least has the decency to look sheepish. He opens his mouth and closes it, speechless for the first time in his life.

With jerking movements, I grab my notebook and pencil from the counter, say a quick goodbye to Julia and Papi, and head for the door without a glance in Jonah's direction.

Stomp, stomp, stomp. I blast my way through the lobby. Of all the ridiculous, idiotic, stupid . . .

"Edmund, wait, don't be mad." Jonah catches up to me by the elevators. "I didn't mean to jinx us. I didn't know!"

I ignore him and step into the elevator. He follows. The door closes behind us. Before he can speak again, I whirl around and put my finger in his face. "I'm going to tell your mother that you messed with the Aztec gods!"

"Mayans," he corrects me in a calm tone.

When I don't respond, he shoves his hands in his pockets and kicks at the floor. "It's just a stupid statue," he mutters.

A loud rumble of thunder shakes the building. The elevator jerks and sways, then shudders to a halt. The lights flicker out.

Silence.

Chapter 7

BE ON GUARD

DAY 8

Yesterday it took them sixty-three minutes and twenty seconds to get the electricity back on. That's sixty-three minutes and twenty seconds stuck in an elevator with a hyperactive kid who just ate a pound of sugar cookies. Not the greatest moment of our friendship, but we made up two hours later. I can't *really* blame him for the bad weather, after all.

The past few days have been pretty dismal, but today is a new day, a *great* day. The word on the street—or at least, in the hallways of the hotel—is that they've arrested someone for the mask robbery. Someone local. Which means they shouldn't be investigating Dad anymore. It's a miracle!

And the sun is shining, not a cloud in sight. This morning we went snorkeling and saw some sea turtles. Totally cool. Then we went into town and had the best chicken tacos I've ever eaten. We may even swim with dolphins later at a nearby water park, although it costs two hundred bucks a person, so maybe not.

"Just one more store," Mom says, pulling me by the arm through the crowded marketplace. Vendors are shouting at us to buy everything from T-shirts to candy skeletons to red, white, and green Mexican flags.

Mom has the weekend off from the conference, and I have to say, it's nice having her around. We split off from Jonah and Dad after lunch, claiming that we needed to do some early Christmas shopping. I thought she just wanted an excuse to have some mother-son bonding time, but she was actually serious and has dragged me to twenty-eight stores and vendor carts.

As for certain Mayan rain gods, Chaac, aka the Statue Formerly Known as Mr. Q, has been washed off, dried, and wrapped in a soft tissue. I wanted to throw him away, but Jonah said that would just make Chaac angry and he'd send a tornado. So we're "pampering" him, trying to lull his rain powers to sleep. It seems to be working.

I follow my mom through the plaza, but a crowd has gathered around a mariachi band, making it hard to move. Sweaty tourist bodies press on me from all sides.

"Let's get out of here!" Mom shouts over the loud trumpet and guitar music. She hates crowds almost as much as I do. She starts to head for a taxi stand, then stops and grins as she stares at the musicians. I follow her line of sight.

Oh . . . no . . .

My father is dancing right in front of the band, as if he's part of the act. His broad chest is draped in a bright red poncho, and there's a huge tan sombrero on his head. He's shaking maracas and his rather ample butt at the same time while the mariachi guys pick up the tempo. And Jonah . . . Jonah's wearing a fake mustache—*I am not kidding*—and is circling my father to the beat, doing spazzy scissor kicks while flapping his arms up and down like an insane bird. The crowd is cheering.

I suck in a mortified breath. Dad and Jonah link arms in time to the music. Dad flips him over his back, and Jonah lands on his feet and bows. Then they break into a Michael Jackson moonwalk, their moves perfectly synchronized, as if they've been practicing for years.

"Let's go, Mom!" I yank on her arm but she drags

her feet, looking over her shoulder at the Mariachi Horror Show.

"But he's so cute," she says.

I know she is *not* referring to Jonah. And for the next year, I'm going to be tortured by her calling my father her handsome dancing *señor* or something equally gross, and I'll be forced to run away to Canada.

Pushing our way through the crowd, we pop out the other side of the plaza, right in front of El Museo Nacional de Arte Moderno, that art museum we visited last weekend.

"Oof!" I say as I collide with a dark-haired man, my shoulder making contact with his spine. He shrugs me off without a glance, his attention focused on the museum in front of him. After jogging up the stone staircase, he pauses at the top to scowl over his shoulder at the person who just stumbled into him. Which would be me.

My heart freezes in my rib cage.

It's *him*.

Ghostman, the pushy tourist from the hotel. The tourist who looks like the dead bank robber. Black hair and tanned skin. *Click.* A thin mustache, gray eyes. *Click.* He's dressed in a maroon uniform, just like the other museum guards. He pulls a handkerchief out of his pocket to mop his brow while speaking to another guard posted by the entrance. I push my glasses up on my nose and squint to get a better view. They seem serious, their heads bent in concentration. Then Ghostman nods and heads through the large glass doors.

Who *is* this guy? Is he really a guard? Or is he just dressed like one? I stop and pretend to tie my sneakers while attempting to get a grip on my brain. *Think, Edmund, think!*

I turn to Mom and break out my best acting skills. "Can we go into the museum?" I gesture to the huge stone building in front of us. "I really want to see those Diego Rivera paintings again. We studied his use of flowers last year in art class, and I know Mrs. Lower will give me extra credit if I do a report on him." When in doubt, bring Improvement of School Grades into the discussion.

She raises an eyebrow. "I thought you were *dying* to get out of here."

"I am. Just for a few minutes." I grab her hand and tug her up the stairs. I need to find this guy. How I'll do that with my mom attached to my side, I have no idea.

She lets me lead the way, but partway up, she stops walking. "It's closed." She points to a small sign ahead that reads CERRADO.

"But it's a Saturday," I say, racking my brain for a good excuse as to why we should press forward. "They must have forgotten to take the sign down this morning. Let's just ask. I really need to see those paintings. Please?" I eyeball the guard posted by the doors. Is he working with Ghostman?

"We'll try," Mom says. Of course she believes me. Partly because I'm flashing her my best *I love you* smile, and partly because she knows I'm an über-nerd who loves to study art for hours at a time.

We climb a few more stairs and the guard steps forward, holding up his hand. *"El museo está cerrado,"* he says in a gruff voice.

"Hi!" Mom says brightly while flashing him a smile that would bring most mortals to their knees. "We were hoping we could take a quick look at the Diego Rivera paintings."

The guard stares at my mom as if he's been hit with a dummy stick. He's tall and thin, his face set in a stern expression. Well, it *was* a stern expression. Now he's blinking a lot and a soft smile curls the corners of his mouth. This is the effect my mother has on people. She thinks it's because she's nice, and maybe that's part of it, but I've seen men and women alike practically throw themselves at her feet because of her striking beauty. High cheekbones, creamy coffee skin, huge brown eyes.

The guard snaps out of it. "It—it is impossible," he stammers in accented English. "There is a new exhibit opening Thursday. We are closed until then. I wish I could let you in, *señora*. I am so sorry." His voice borders on desperate, as if her disappointment is crushing his world.

"Okay," Mom says kindly. "Thank you for your help." She turns to go.

And I know that's the end of that.

Defeated, I tromp down the steps. She pats my back. "We'll come back next week for the new exhibit," she says. "Are you okay, honey? You look like you've seen a ghost."

Chapter 8

BIG BREAK

—

ONE HOUR LATER

I learned how to ride a bike two years ago at Camp Little Hiawatha. Jonah and I spent a week in the Catskills, where we hiked and examined fox scat (a fancy word for poop) and were eaten alive by mosquitoes. Our counselor, Jerry—a nice guy who made his own granola that tasted like honey, gravel, and twigs—took it upon himself to teach us city kids how to ride, and I haven't practiced since. We ride scooters in Central Park since there's zero space in our apartments to store bikes.

I'm thinking about Jerry and his break-your-teeth granola as I push a rental bike up the steep hill into town with Julia, wondering how badly I'm going to embarrass myself.

"My cousin is innocent," Julia says. She walks beside me, shoving her bike forward with an angry push. When Mom and I returned to the hotel, we bumped into a very upset Julia. It turns out that the local guy the police arrested is her cousin Miguel, a sixteen-year-old waiter who works at the hotel. We met him last week and he seemed perfectly normal.

"Why did they arrest him?" I ask. "He's just a kid. I thought they were looking for a man with a mustache." I puff out the words through choppy breaths. Am I really this out of shape? I blame the heat. You could fry an egg on the sidewalk.

"It's all Capitán Ruiz," she says bitterly. "The police received an anonymous tip about Las Plumas. Someone called to say that the gang has a new leader, a leader who is planning something big. So Ruiz blames Las Plumas for the robbery. And Miguel . . . Miguel used to be a Pluma."

What? That's crazy. But when I examine the picture of Miguel in my mind, I can see it clearly: a black feather tattoo on his wrist, partially hidden beneath a leather bracelet. I should have caught that detail when I first met him. I'm losing my edge.

And Las Plumas have a new leader? Could it be Ghostman? I keep my question to myself, instead saying, "Miguel used to be a Pluma? He's not anymore?"

She nods, her eyes focused on the road ahead. "He joined when he was thirteen but left after a year. He's a good boy. He'd never steal our family's mask." Her voice rises. "My father needs to come home. He needs to fix this. But the roads and bridges are so damaged from the storm. He's stuck!"

"I can help you," I say as my brain officially disconnects from my mouth. "I'm a professional. I've done this kind of thing before."

She looks at me, blinking her huge, pretty eyes. Am I really going to tell her about being Eddie Red and break the NYPD contract I signed? She seems trustworthy.

"What do you mean?" she demands.

So I tell her. I tell her how I have a photographic memory and I witnessed a crime back in New York and drew an awesome picture of the bad guy. How I got hired by the NYPD as Eddie Red and how Jonah and I foiled the plans of a criminal mastermind. I talk and talk and talk, watching her face go from surprised to disbelieving to impressed. Then back to disbelieving.

"Look," I say, practically tripping over my feet as I push the bike along. "I wish I had a badge to flash you or some kind of proof, but I don't. And you can't tell anyone about this. But I promise, just because my dad's off the hook doesn't mean I'm off the case. We'll figure this out."

She examines me, her gaze like a laser. Finally she nods. "Okay." She comes to a sudden stop. We've arrived at the top of the hill.

Throwing her leg over her bike, she says, "Let's pedal through the marketplace. Then we'll ride by the museum a few times."

Back at the hotel, I had told her about my Ghostman sighting, and we agreed that returning to the museum immediately was the best plan. Mom thinks we're doing a "cultural bike tour."

I'm not sure what we'll do if we actually catch Ghostman, but I'm running with the plan. Or biking with it, as is the case right now. Time to put my Little Hiawatha skills to the test.

Clipping on my helmet, I scan the road, looking for potential hazards. I wish Jonah were here. I keep calling his cell, but it goes straight to voicemail. I wonder if the American Dancing Duo is still hanging out with their mariachi buddies. The plaza is pretty empty at the moment. It's siesta time, when everyone takes a huge nap in the heat of the day.

Julia takes off, an obvious biking pro. She zips

down the narrow street, past a few tourists and rusty cars, weaving her way through the market vendors with grace. After a shaky push-off, I get my bike going and almost crash into a fruit cart. I start up again, wobbling around a man selling woven blankets. I have to pedal hard to catch up to her, and right when I start to get the hang of it, we stop by the museum steps. No sign of Ghostman anywhere.

"There's an exhibit of Aztec gold coming," Julia says, pointing to a big banner that reads ORO AZTECA. Why did I not see that before? The blazing sun must really be affecting my observation skills.

"Let's check out the alley behind the plaza," she says. "There's a back entrance to the museum there."

My pulse speeds up. The last time I was in an alley, I was held at gunpoint and duct-taped to a drainpipe. I *hate* alleys.

While I hesitate, she takes off, zooming past the museum to hook a left down the alley. Suddenly she skids to a halt in a spray of pebbles and spins the bike around in a cool maneuver that I have no hope of imitating. My mouth drops open in surprise as she pedals back toward me like a madwoman.

"*¡Chica!*" a group of teen punks yells at her. They've just come running out of the alley at a full sprint. Do

they recognize Julia? They seem to. *"¡Chica!"* they call
again.

There are three of them: a tattooed kid leads the
charge, with two beefier guys right on his heels. *Click*
goes the camera in my mind. Tan skin — *click* — gold-
capped teeth — *click* — black bracelets — *click* —
swirling tattoos. They're heading this way. Fast.

Julia reaches me first. *"¡Rápido,* Edmund! Hurry!"
She flies past me, not pausing to explain. "Las Plumas!" she yells over her shoulder. "Las *Pluummaaas!"*

Never have I been so terrified to hear the word
feather in my life.

I yank my bike around and slam my feet down on
the pedals with a scramble of panicked limbs. *You can
do this. Eyes forward, don't look down, pump your legs.*

"¡Chico!" they yell behind me. Oh, no. *Chico* means
"boy." They saw that I'm with Julia and now they're
going to grab me and cover me with cow's blood or
spray paint or whatever they do to kids they catch.

Faster, Edmund! Faster!

I sway at first but then really get going, adrenaline
streaming through my muscles and granting me a
Moment of Athletic Ability. I zigzag around vending
carts, dodge tourists with ease. More speed. I dare to
peek over my shoulder. The boys have stopped run-

ning, unable to keep up. *Ha! Eat my dust, Feathers Gang!*

I turn back in time to realize that I am going really, really, *really* fast, heading straight down the ginormous hill that I huffed up just ten minutes ago. I try to hit the brakes by slamming my feet on the pedals. The pedals spin backwards wildly. *Not that kind of bike!* I scream at my stupid brain. I squeeze the hand brake, but it's too late.

A dip in the pavement. A patch of sand. I swerve and skid and hit the curb hard with my tire. The bike flips up, up . . .

And over.

Chapter 9

PACO EL GATO

DAY 9

Let me start by saying I'm on pain medication and my brain is a little fuzzy. Plus I smell chocolate . . . *Yum.* And doughnuts . . . *Yum.*

"You're making really weird noises," Jonah says, squinting at me beside the pool. We're sitting in some lounge chairs under the shade of a palm tree, mulling over the latest developments in our case. I look down at my scribbled notes:

-Who is the new leader of Las Plumas?
-Is the Aztec gold exhibit at museum important?
-Is Ghostman planning to rob museum?

It's hard to focus. Mostly I just stare blankly off into space and eat french fries covered in powdered sugar (the medicine's giving me a crazy sweet tooth).

Yesterday my mom and I spent an hour in the emergency room with Julia acting as translator. My left wrist has a small hairline fracture and my knees are pretty scraped up, but it could have been *a lot* worse. It could have been my right hand, my drawing hand. I told Mom it didn't hurt. And I *certainly* didn't mention the chase scene with Las Plumas. She'd never have let me leave the hotel unchaperoned again.

Jonah rustles the pages of his notebook, his head bent in concentration. He's drawn maps showing the location of all the "employees only" rooms, along with color-coded charts of current and former employees, their street addresses, and police records. Two days ago, he finally hacked into the computer system and discovered that a kitchen worker was brought in for questioning twenty years ago for suspicious Plumas activity. Apparently that street gang has been around forever.

"What's the connection?" Jonah mutters at his notes. He shifts in his chair and rubs Mr. Q absent-mindedly with his thumb. The statue is now wearing a red mini-sombrero purchased from a street vendor. After the mariachi show yesterday, Jonah and my dad went to a karaoke club to sing cheesy eighties songs. They couldn't hear their cell phones when we tried to reach them from the clinic—too busy "perfecting their dance moves" to loud music. No comment.

"Are you sure the museum guard was the guy from the lobby?" he asks. "I mean, did you get a good look at his face? Because—"

"It was him." I may be foggy, but I know what I saw.

Jonah sighs. "Well, he's definitely our number one suspect. He was dressed as a tourist the day before the mask was stolen, and now he's dressed as a museum guard when there's an exhibit of Aztec gold coming to town. Very fishy. But I don't get why he looks like a dead bank robber from thirty years ago, or how he's linked to Las Plumas." He scratches his head. "The pieces are all here. We're just not seeing the big picture."

I nod. What can I say? I have nothing to add. I'm almost out of french fries and I really want some chocolate cake. Or maybe some of those Mexican wedding cookies that Papi made the other day. I'd even try some jiggly flan. But Jonah will freak out if I mention food again, so I stare at the sparkling blue pool in front of us and pretend to contemplate the Ghostman mystery.

I can't swim today because the waterproof cast on my arm has to set for twenty-four hours. The outer layer of the cast is bright orange, the only color that was available, so now I look like I have a traffic cone glued to my hand. Not exactly good camouflage for detective work.

"No, I don't have any food!" Jonah swats away a cat that's wandered over to beg. Ever since the storm came and went, the pool complex has been overrun by cats of all kinds. Small and big, fluffy and scrawny. All annoying, all pure evil.

Back home we have a cat named Sadie who is the devil herself cloaked in fur. She and I have been enemies since day one. You may think I'm a terrible person for disliking cats, but let me ask you this: Would *you* like cats if your cat ate your beloved hamster and then left the eyeballs on your pillow? Or if she peed on your backpack but you didn't know it until someone in math class said, "Hey, what smells like cat pee?"

No, you would not.

"Shoo!" I say to a brown cat that's trying to jump up on the end of my chair. I wave my hand at it, forgetting that my wrist is in a cast, and wince at the sudden pain. From out of nowhere, a beat-up old gray cat leaps onto the end of my lounge chair and hisses at the others. They scramble away with their tails tucked between their legs. I smile. Finally a cat I can get on board with.

He—I think it's a he—jumps down and stands at attention at the end of the chair, as if he's guarding me. His tail is crooked and gnarled, one of his eyes is stuck shut, and a huge scar runs over the left side of his face. He could totally pull off a black eye patch. Clearly this cat has seen a lot of action. I open my art pad and start to sketch him.

"I'm not hallucinating this, am I?" I say to Jonah, gesturing to the pirate cat. "There's a one-eyed cat sitting there, right?"

Jonah stares at me as if I've lost all brain cells.

"How you doing, *muchacho*?" Papi's deep voice booms across the pool deck. He's weaving his way through the chairs, dressed in street clothes. I guess he's done with work for the day.

"I'm okay." I smile and show him my sketching hand, not a scratch on it. "I can still draw, don't worry." I've finished three of the five pictures he wants me to do. I think he'll like them.

PACO

"Muy bien." He winks at me, then looks down at the cat by my feet. "Hey, Paco," he says. The cat hisses in response and Papi chuckles. "Always so *maleducado.* So rude. He likes you, though, gringo." His deep laugh follows him off the patio.

An orange cat slinks under my chair, no doubt smelling the last of my fries, which are resting by my flip-flops. With a sudden flurry of claws, Paco bats at him, sending the would-be thief fleeing across the deck. Paco pauses to sniff my food but then resumes his post at the end of my chair. I grab the greasy paper container and dump the scraps on the ground. "Here you go," I call to him. He eyeballs me with his good eye, then trots over to chow down. I swear he salutes me with his tail.

"—listening to me?" Jonah snaps.

"What?"

He frowns at me, then at Paco. Then his face lights up like the Fourth of July as Julia strolls onto the pool deck. She's quite official-looking in her cargo shorts and white collared shirt with the hotel emblem on the pocket. She waves at us and taps her watch. Huh?

Jonah stands up and starts shoving his books into his bag. "We're going," he announces. "Your parents are taking us to the island. It's perfect. We need to check out the Plumas crime scene at the top of the pyramid. We don't know why the Plumas went after Julia yesterday, and we have to figure out how it's all connected." He throws my T-shirt at my head. "Get dressed. This case isn't solved and Julia needs us."

"All right." I fumble with my shirt and end up with my head through an armhole. In my defense, I'm a bit uncoordinated from the meds plus things are tricky with this cast on my arm.

After watching me struggle a moment, Jonah tugs my shirt around to help me find the right hole. Then he shakes his head and flips on his aviator shades. "Just say no to drugs, Edmund. Just say no."

Chapter 10

EL CAPITÁN

———

FORTY-THREE MINUTES LATER

"The Mayans built pyramids in what is now Mexico, Honduras, Belize, and Guatemala," Julia says in a tour-guide voice. "The pyramids have steep staircases on two or four sides and were used for sacrificial rituals."

I nod as I sketch, attempting to draw the enormous pyramid that we're standing on.

"Actually," Dad says, "they built two types of pyramids. One with stairs and one without. The ones without a staircase were completely sacred and off-limits to the people." His mustache twitches the way it does when he's getting excited about history.

"I've been researching Chichén Itzá for my novel," he continues. "Did you know there's a sports field there? The Mayans played a game with a soccer-sized ball in front of huge crowds of spectators. Of course," he chuckles, "sometimes the losers were beheaded."

Julia nods politely. "Yes, I have heard that." I can't tell if she's irritated by his interruption. I wish he and my mom would leave so we could check out the Plumas crime scene, but they keep hanging around, taking pictures of the ocean.

I admit the view from up here is incredible. We can see for miles in all directions. In front of us, long white beaches extend along the mainland, framed by palm trees and towering hotels. And behind us the turquoise ocean stretches on forever. Jonah's in heaven, interrupting Julia to talk about war tactics and the Spanish Armada and how cool it would be to do battle from up here. He's been obsessed with military stuff practically since birth.

Julia's not impressed. "You will notice," she continues in a stern tone after telling Jonah that this temple was *not* used for war purposes, "that the top of this pyramid is flat. This is how the Mayans constructed all of their pyramids. It is because they always built a temple on the top. The temple was used not only for religious ceremonies, but also to observe the stars. The Mayans were very advanced in astronomy."

"I bet they used it for war, too," Jonah says, hopping back and forth excitedly. "You can really see your enemies coming from up here. Do you think they shot arrows at the Spaniards when they arrived in boats? I bet they did."

Jonah has a secret plan for getting rid of my parents, and he ordered me not to interfere. No interrupting, no speaking of any kind. I'm the dumb bystander who's been assigned a few random tasks, such as storing his water in my backpack and drawing pictures of the pyramid. Because I'm on pain meds, I have been deemed "a liability."

"The Mayan civilization was already disappearing by the time the Spanish arrived here!" Julia says in exasperation.

Mom sighs beside me. If anyone can drive her away from a beautiful view, it's Jonah. As Jonah and Julia continue to bicker and Dad interjects a random factoid when he can, I sketch the crumbling temple in front of us. Any minute now, my mother will grab my dad and head down the steep stairs. Any minute now . . .

"All I'm saying is that it's possible that the Mayans and Spaniards met up," Jonah says in a loud voice.

"And therefore it's possible that the Mayans saw the Spanish ships coming from up here. And therefore it's possible they used this for military defense."

Julia throws her hands up in the air and lets loose a bunch of Spanish, the words popping like firecrackers. I catch an *estúpido* and maybe a *bobo*.

Mom sighs again and slides her camera into her purse. "Dad and I want to check out the gift shop," she tells me. "We'll see you kids down there." She takes Dad's hand and practically drags him down the stairs. I can tell he doesn't want to go. I think he was actually getting into the Mayan military debate.

"Sure thing, Mrs. L," Jonah calls after her. He keeps a fake smile on his face a few heartbeats more. Then his mouth folds into a frown. "I thought they'd never leave. All right, troops, fan out and canvas the area. No detail is too small." He salutes us, his eyes a bit manic. You don't want to get in Jonah's way when he's in Serious Soldier Mode.

We walk carefully and slowly around the temple. I take it all in, snapping pictures in my mind of every detail. I'm much more alert now. During the boat ride over, I stuck my head far over the railing so I wouldn't get seasick. It worked, the cool ocean spray refreshing me, bringing me out of my pain-medication fog. I am back in the game.

Two questions are on my mind as I examine every inch of the stone: Is this Plumas crime scene related to the stolen mask? And how does Ghostman tie in?

It's actually not much of a crime scene, not anymore. The blood is gone, washed away by all of Chaac's rain. I walk along the worn rock, skirting the perimeter. The first two walls are mostly rubble, the third standing tall with the word *muerte* written in blue spray paint.

"*Muerte* means 'death,' right?" Jonah says to Julia.

She scowls at the graffiti. "Yes. It's some kind of political message. They hate the government, hate the police, hate anyone with power."

"Looks like they hate somebody named A," I say, pointing to wall number four, where the letter *A* is sprayed in blue. Julia shrugs and moves on, frowning down at the ground. The temple floor is smashed in places, as if somebody took a sledgehammer to the rock. Is it recent destruction by Las Plumas, or just the product of centuries of sun and wind?

"Why would they do this?" Julia says, pointing to the broken stones. "This was a beautiful floor marked with hieroglyphics. Now it is destroyed."

THE TEMPLE

Jonah squats down and shifts the stones to reveal packed-down dirt. "Is there anything under here?" he asks.

Julia nods. "A tomb. My great-grandfather was the archaeologist who discovered a hidden chamber inside. It made him famous." There's pride in her voice. "The treasure was removed," she adds, no doubt seeing Jonah's excited treasure-hunter expression. "The tomb was sealed off. It is empty." She shakes her head, kicking at the rubble. "Las Plumas have gone too far this time."

Jonah continues to poke at the dirt, humming the theme song from Indiana Jones. I circle the temple once more, then perch on a stone step to sketch what I've seen. A fat gray iguana suns itself on a nearby rock.

After a few minutes, Jonah sits down beside me and pulls a wad of key chains out of his pocket. Chaac, aka Mr. Q, is clipped to a bunch of other junk: a miniature ninja sword, a New York Yankees medallion, and a flat green square that reads I SUR-VIVED THE ALIEN INVASION. How Jonah fits it all in his pocket is beyond me.

"Chaac needs some air," he explains as he separates the small stone statue from the tangle of metal. "He needs to get back to his Mayan roots." He strokes him lovingly on the stomach. Then he pulls out another tiny statue, Chaac's new buddy, Ah Puch (pronounced "Ah Pwash"). He's the Mayan god of death and is beyond creepy with his saggy skin and bulging eyeballs. He's also known as The Flatulent One, which is why Jonah bought him. (*Flatulent* means "gassy," in case you didn't know.) Jonah claims that not only will Ah Puch be a fierce and loyal friend to Mr. Q, but he'll also make him laugh with his farts, and laughter is the key to a good friendship.

I try to stay on task. "What do you think of the *A*?" I say, gesturing to the wall beside us.

He shrugs. "Maybe they were going to paint another word but had to leave in a hurry?"

"Yeah, I was thinking that too," I say. "Death to someone. Wishing death on someone whose name starts with an *A*? Some kind of political message?"

Jonah shrugs again. He rubs his cheek and stares at the ocean. "Why would the Plumas smash the temple floor?" he says. "Were they trying to get into the tomb?"

I've been wondering that same thing. I'm about to answer when I see a group of men marching up the pyramid steps. I stand up in surprise. Captain Ruiz is leading the charge. What's he doing here? Is he spying on my family? I wonder if Dad bumped into him down at the bottom.

Jonah moves like a skittish animal, shoving the statues in his pocket and scrambling over to Julia just as Ruiz makes it to the top. Even in the ocean breeze, Ruiz's hair is slicked back and tidy. He sees me and his mouth opens in angry shock. It's not illegal to be up here, is it?

Julia steps into view from behind the temple wall, her arms folded. *"Capitán,"* she greets him coolly. I can tell it's taking a lot of her self-control to remain calm, considering what he's done to her cousin.

He shifts his piercing glare from me to her and starts to rattle on in Spanish with bossy hand gestures. I have no idea what he's saying, but he points to the temple walls and then to a pair of men who are lugging some kind of tube-shaped machine up the stairs.

He glances at me again and his tone changes, lower and scolding. *"No debes estar con ellos,"* he says to her. I swear he's just slowed down his Spanish so that I can understand him. *"Su padre está en la lista de sospechosos."*

Wait a minute. *Padre* means "father," and *lista*

97

means "list," and I suspect *sospechosos* means "suspects." Is he saying that Julia shouldn't be hanging out with us because my father's on the list of suspects? But that can't be right, can it? I must have heard him wrong. Maybe the medication's still messing with my mind.

Julia tosses me a nervous glance. And I know that I understood their conversation just fine.

My father is still a suspect.

After one last burst of rapid-fire Spanish, Ruiz saunters off, yapping at his men.

"We have to go," Julia tells me. "They are going to clean up the mess and erase the graffiti. I don't understand why Ruiz is here. This is a job for the temple curator, not the police." She frowns, as if surprised she actually voiced her worries out loud. "Don't worry about your father," she adds quickly. "I'm sure he will be cleared soon."

Yeah, right.

The three of us trudge down the steep steps. We didn't really learn anything new here. Nothing to tie the crime to Ghostman or to connect Las Plumas with the Mayan mask.

Captain Ruiz jogs past us, bumping me out of the

way—on my bad cast arm, no less—as if he owns the stairs. My blood boils just looking at him. He's arrogant, cruel, and ready to arrest the wrong man to promote his own career. I have to stop him.

"We need to up our game," I say to Jonah.

Chapter 11

OPERATION COUSIN JUAN

DAY 10

"Are you sure you know what you're doing?" I say.

"Of course. I'm a professional." Jonah dabs glue on my upper lip, then presses a thin black mustache onto my skin. This is not what I had in mind when we talked about upping our game yesterday.

"I'll be right back. Don't look," he commands. As if I could. He took my glasses off and refuses to give them back. Not until he's done "creating his masterpiece." I glance in the mirror, but all I see is a dark blur.

This all started after breakfast, when we spotted the clerk behind the front desk. *The* clerk, the young guy who was working in the lobby last week when the mask was stolen. He looked thinner, with dark circles under his eyes, and when the birds squawked, he jumped like a gun had gone off. He was nervous, twitchy, and tired: the perfect candidate for an interrogation.

So now Jonah's preparing a disguise for a secret mission, and yours truly is going undercover. I haven't come up with a better plan, so I'm going with it.

I squint at the fake badge in my hand. On one side is a gold eagle with a CIA emblem, and on the other is a clear plastic sleeve with a photo ID Jonah found on the street last year. He was saving it for a special occasion.

"Victor Muellenthorpe?" I say, reading the name beneath the photo. According to the card, Victor is a thirty-three-year-old male with curly black hair and a mustache (of course) living in Brooklyn. He's thin and has dark brown skin like me, but the similarities end there.

"That's you," Jonah responds in a chipper voice.

Do not panic, do not panic. There is *no* way we can pull this off. I wonder what the penalty is down here for impersonating an officer of the law. Serious jail time for sure. *Do not panic.*

Jonah's back, crowding my personal space. "We need to rehearse your lines," he says while fussing with my new mustache. His fingers smell like peanut butter.

"No, you'll just make me nervous. It has to flow naturally." I squirm away from his hand. "I've got it under control. I'm doing the Cousin John trick."

Even without my glasses on, I can tell he's staring at me blankly, so I clarify: "Remember I told you about the Cousin John thing I saw on that cop show? How everyone has a Cousin John?" It's true—I have one on my dad's side who lives in Atlanta. I think Jonah has one in Ohio.

"Yeah, so?"

"So everyone down here must have a Cousin Juan. The clerk doesn't look very bright. He should fall for it." If he believes I'm a thirty-three-year-old CIA agent, that is. I scratch at the mustache. Jonah bats my hand away.

"Don't touch," he scolds. "Here, put this on." He shoves my arm into a jacket sleeve. It takes me a moment to realize it's his father's tan trench coat. His dad's a small guy, so we only have to fold the cuffs up once.

"Can I have my glasses back?" I say.

"In a minute. And you'll be using your prescription sunglasses, not your regular ones. Lean forward," he says. I obey, and he pulls something tight over my skull. A wig of some kind. He owns some really sketchy wigs. Mohawks, bald monks, rainbow clowns . . . *Do not panic.*

"There," he says, pride in his voice. He hands me my sunglasses. Hastily I shove them on and turn to look in the mirror.

A black curly wig. The perfect mustache. Stage makeup that shades my skin for an older look. A trench coat buttoned up to my neck. With my dark shades, I *am* Victor Muellenthorpe. A short Victor Muellenthorpe, but a believable one all the same.

Jonah helps me into a pair of black leather gloves. We're going with gloves to complete the look because first of all, I have an orange cast on my left wrist, and second of all, my fingers look like they belong to a second grader. Then he motions toward the door. "All right, Mr. M," he says. "Show time."

Five minutes later I'm marching through the lobby with long strides that I hope appear manly and confident. Jonah's already in place, hiding around the corner of the lobby desk behind a potted plant. My heart is pounding like crazy.

Relax! I scold myself. I've had harder acting parts before. Last year our class did a production of *Our*

Town, and I played an old milkman who talked to invisible cows. Everyone said it was the most inspiring performance of the show. If I can do that, I can do this.

And at least I'm not worried about bumping into my parents. Mom's at her conference and Dad's in his room, happily typing away on his novel (working title: *Oh My, Mayans!*). He thinks we've already left for Julia's house. We'll leave as soon as we're done here, assuming we're not arrested first.

I approach the desk. The clerk is fiddling with his tie. He's young, maybe early twenties, with short brown hair, and he's blinking his eyes as if he's nervous. Good. I need to keep him that way, keep him off-balance so he doesn't have time to think. Thinking leads to suspicion leads to him realizing I'm just a kid.

"Luis Gusto?" I say in a deep voice. I have the sudden urge to giggle.

"Y-yes?" Luis stammers. Blink, blink. He looks me up and down, taking in the bizarrely short man before him.

"Victor Muellenthorpe, CIA." I flash my plastic badge. "Your cousin Juan is in trouble with the law.

But today's your lucky day. I can help him, if you help me."

"Juanito?" he says. "But he is at university. How—?"

"People get into trouble at university, don't they." I slap my hand on the desk. A satisfying *smack* of leather glove on marble counter echoes in the lobby. Luis flinches at the sudden noise. "I need to know what happened here the day the Mayan mask was stolen," I demand.

He runs a hand over his short hair. "I already told the police."

"Now the CIA is involved. Tell me what happened and I'll help you with Juan."

I must be convincing, because the guy spills his guts right away. He talks fast about how he was on duty and got a phone call that there was a package at the back door. The lobby was empty at the time, so he decided to take a quick break and get it. When he returned, the mask was gone.

"The package was just a piece of paper," Luis explains in a squeaky voice. I feel sorry for the guy. "I did not mean to be irresponsible."

"What was on the paper?"

"The words *Danke schön,* written in big letters."

"Danke schön?" I let out a kidlike gasp, momentarily breaking character. My mind is reeling. Why would someone write the German term for *thank you*? Luis is staring at me, no longer blinking. Oops, I need to get back on track here.

I slap my hand on the counter again. "Tell me about the caller," I say. "Did he have an accent? Was he Mexican?"

"N-no," Luis stammers. "I mean, he was not Mexican, but his Spanish was perfect. I don't . . . eh . . . maybe he had a slight German accent."

What is it with me and German bad guys?

"Who did you say you were?" Luis asks in a stronger voice. A suspicious voice. Time to go.

I wave him off. "Don't worry about it. You never saw me." I turn to leave, being sure to keep my steps steady and smooth. "And don't worry about Juan," I call over my shoulder. "He'll be fine." I walk around the corner. As soon as I'm out of sight, I sprint for the exit without a glance at Jonah's hiding spot.

Outside the front door, I dive behind some thick green bushes and rip off the gloves, wig, and trench coat with shaking fingers. Jonah joins me a moment later.

"That was *awesome!*" He slaps me on the back.

"Did you see Luis? What's he doing?" I say.

He holds out a backpack for me to shove the costume into. "He's fine. Confused, but fine. He's helping some lady with her keycard."

I breathe out in relief. "Give me a second, okay?" I need to collect myself before we go to Julia's.

He nods. "I'll grab us a cab." The bushes shake as he wades through them.

I sit on the ground, my skin on fire as I peel the mustache off. Ouch! I rub my upper lip, contemplating what I've just learned. I know I should be happy I just pulled off this stunt, but I'm not. The new information doesn't make any sense. Was it Ghostman who left the note? Why would he write it in German? Maybe it's not him at all. Maybe the Plumas have been broadening their horizons and taking foreign language classes.

Something soft rubs against my leg and I nearly jump out of my skin.

"You scared me!" I scold Paco the cat. He purrs in response, flicking his tail back and forth with a lazy swish. His purr is like thunder, crackly and uneven. There are streaks on his neck, hairless scars where he probably damaged his voice box in a fight. Coolest cat ever.

I scratch him behind the ear and realize that he's chewing on something. Something white.

"Whatcha got there, boy?" I fish a wet glob out of his mouth. Ugh. Wet feathers. "Did you eat a bird?" I ask. He answers by rubbing his body against my leg again. I pet him one more time and head over to the taxi stand, where Jonah's waiting. A bunch of white feathers lie scattered on the ground, like a mini bird-bomb went off. Clearly Paco's been busy.

I stop in my tracks. White feathers on the ground . . . White feathers on the ground . . .

I stare and stare, pieces clicking into place.

Bingo.

Chapter 12

COPY CAT

FIFTEEN MINUTES LATER

"We have a copy cat," I announce to Julia. We're at her house, sitting on the couch in her father's office. I already went through my copy cat theory with Jonah during the cab ride here, and he's on board. Currently he's over at the desk, quietly sifting through crime scene photos of Las Plumas.

Julia wrinkles her forehead. "A what?"

"A copy cat. Someone is trying to imitate the crimes of Las Plumas." I pull out my notebook. "Here's a list of what the Plumas' crime scenes contain." I flip partway through my notes and hold the pad up for her:

Elements of Plumas' Crime Scenes
-Cow's blood
-Graffiti

"Okay," she says, biting her lip as she tries to piece it all together.

I tap on the page with my pencil. "When we went out to the island the first time, I saw what I thought were white flower petals stuck in the blood. But they weren't petals, they were feathers. Someone put feathers at the crime scene!"

She stares at me. The Moment of Enlightenment is not coming.

"Jonah," I say. "Can we please have Exhibit A?"

"Yep." He hands me a photo from the desk. It's a bloody scene of a statue in town, one of the photos Julia showed me last week. "This picture was taken a year ago," I explain, pointing to the date in the corner. "Not a feather in sight, right?"

She nods, so I continue. "In last week's attack on the temple, there were feathers. Someone staged a Plumas crime scene. That person mistakenly thought that the Plumas leave feathers at their crime scenes. Get it?"

Her eyes light up with understanding. "But why? Why do this?"

"I have a theory. The temple vandalism and the stolen mask occurred the same morning. What if someone planted the Plumas crime scene over on the island and then stole the mask while the police were distracted?"

"Just like Pablo Valero did thirty years ago!" she exclaims. "If Ghostman is Pablo's son, then it makes sense he would imitate his father's work." She pauses. "I still don't understand why they arrested Miguel."

"The day the mask was stolen, there was a lot of chaos," I explain. "There were a few feathers on the lobby floor, but I assumed they had fallen from the blue birds who live there." I flip through the pages of my notebook and show her the pictures I drew of the lobby right after the crime took place. "But now that I look at the pictures in my mind, I see that the feathers are white. They're the same white feathers that were stuck in the blood on the pyramid. Whoever is imitating Las Plumas is also framing them for the stolen mask!"

Julia touches the picture, her finger tracing the feathers I drew on the floor by the empty glass case. "My cousin Miguel is an ex-Pluma, and he was at the hotel that day, so he's taking the blame."

I nod. It all makes sense. Everything except my father as a suspect. What does he have to do with any of this?

"Why are they called the Feathers Gang, anyway?"

Jonah says, thrumming his fingers on the desk. *Tap-tap-tappity-tap.*

Julia sighs. "Miguel said the feather is for fallen angels. They claim they are good kids having to do bad because they think the local government is corrupt." She waves a hand in the air. "They are foolish." Taking the notebook from me, she examines the list while chewing on the end of a pen.

Tap-tappity-tap. The sound of Jonah's busy fingers fills the silence. He mumbles to himself while staring down at the photos, his hands wandering over the wooden surface of the desk as if they have a mind of their own. *Tap-tap-bang!* He's found a jar of pens and has pulled two out, using them as drumsticks.

Julia stands up and removes a small glass angel that's sitting beside the jar of pens. She places it on a shelf above us. Smart move.

Uncapping her pen, she sits back down beside me. "You forgot one thing," she says, scribbling something on my Plumas list. I can't help it, I tense up. *She's only trying to help,* I scold myself. *She can write in your notebook.* I look over her shoulder to see what she's added to the list:

—No smashed stone

"The Plumas do not destroy the landmarks," she explains. "But our copy cat smashed the temple floor. Why? Was it just a mistake, like the feathers?"

I scratch my head. Another question with no answer. "Can we look at the file again on that bank robbery from thirty years ago?" I say. "Maybe there's a clue there." I doubt it, but I need to look at *something*. Jonah's hogging the Plumas photos, hunched over them like a gargoyle.

Julia lugs out the thick police file and flips it open, the newspaper article entitled *El oro está con mi niño* resting at the top. " 'The gold is with my son,' " I say. "You said that the bank robber didn't have a son, right?"

"There is none on record. That is why it was such a huge mystery." She brushes a stray piece of hair off her forehead. "Everyone in the country searched for the mysterious *niño*. Find the *niño*, find the gold." She shrugs. "My father gave up years ago. It is a . . . what's the expression? A cold case."

I stare at the newspaper article. Ghostman looks so much like the robber in the mug shot. *Definitely* his son. I clear my throat. "What if the son was born in a different country? Like . . . Germany, for example." I don't mention the Victor Muellenthorpe stunt. I'm not sure how Julia would react, being the daughter of the police chief and all. "Did the police search foreign birth records?"

"I don't know," she says. "We can ask my father when he returns."

"When's he coming back?" My voice is dangerously close to squeaking. We need him here. We need him to answer questions about my dad.

She shuffles through the newspaper clippings, scanning the articles with lightning speed. "Tonight, I hope. My mother says his cell must have died, because her calls go straight to voicemail."

"Oh." We only have four days left to solve this. What if they don't let my dad leave the country with us? Can they do that? What if we get kicked out of Mexico but he's forced to stay here?

"MAM!" Jonah shouts the bizarre word as he slams his palms down on the desk with a loud thud.

To Julia's credit, she doesn't even flinch at the sudden outburst. Nerves of steel, this girl.

Jonah whirls around with a handful of photos, scattering the rest to the ground. "The copy cat is leaving a message!" He shoves the photos onto our laps. "Look at this. The Plumas always wrote a word or a phrase, things like 'Death to the Government' and stuff like that. But look at the three most recent sites. They're the only ones with feathers, and there's always an extra letter off to the side. An *A* at the temple. An *M* two weeks ago at the market. And another *M* last month by the cultural center. *MMA* . . . Mam? What does it mean?"

The room falls strangely silent. It's as if all the oxygen has been sucked out of our breathing space.

"Ghostman's not done," he continues. "He's telling the cops where his final crime is going to take place. He's playing with them!"

"This isn't Lars, Jonah," I say, referring to Lars Heinrich, the crazy art thief we stopped in New York two months ago. Lars loved leaving complicated clues to where he was going to strike next. A total psycho.

"These letters could be initials," Jonah says. "AMM, MMA, MAM. Oh! The Mexican art museum in town. That's MAM — that's where he's going to strike!" He jumps up and punches a fist in the air like he's solved everything and has already caught the bad guy.

Julia shakes her head. "Those initials are MNAM. They mean Museo Nacional de Arte Moderno. We're missing an *N*."

Jonah grabs the photos off our laps, his brow scrunched in determination. "I'll find it. It has to be here somewhere. That's his target, I can feel it. The upcoming exhibit is Aztec gold! Of *course* he's going to rob the museum!"

He bends down to scoop the photos off the floor. "Help me look. We need to find an *N*." He glances up at us. "We need to . . ." The words die in his throat. He's completely frozen, his eyes wide with fear, like a deer about to be plowed over by a Mac truck.

I follow his line of sight behind me. A man is standing in the office doorway. A man with angry eyes, a tired face, and a large gun belt loaded with weapons. He stares at us, then at the mess of photos and newspaper articles strewn about the office. Then back at us.

"Hola, Papá," Julia says in a small voice.

Chapter 13

LAS PLUMAS

———

DAY 11

"Your dad was pretty mad," I say to Julia the next morning as we wind our way through the busy marketplace. We took a cab into town—no more bikes for us—and are going to scour every inch of this place until we find Ghostman.

She shrugs. "I've seen worse. And he is grateful for your drawing, so that helps."

After her father's initial freak-out (being yelled at in a foreign language is über-scary), Julia managed to calm him down long enough to show him the picture I drew of Ghostman. He was impressed, really impressed, and promised to get to the bottom of this whole mess. He also ordered us to halt our investigation and leave the police work to the police.

So naturally we're staking out the museum.

"And you told him about the Germany connection?" I press her. "That we think Ghostman might be German?"

She smiles and nods. Last night after dinner, we confessed the whole Victor Muellenthorpe thing to her. She thought it was great, a cool spy maneuver. There's a lot more to this nice girl than meets the eye.

The gray stone steps of the museum loom ahead. My pulse quickens. It's time to catch a bad guy.

"We've got to get in there," Jonah says, eyeballing the CERRADO sign and the guard standing out front by the glass doors.

"Let's go through the alley," Julia suggests. "There's a service door back there for museum deliveries. Maybe it's open."

Jonah nods and starts to follow her toward the alley entrance. Once again, I hesitate, not quite able to make myself step into an alley. I still have nightmares about being taped to that stupid alley drainpipe, watching helplessly as my carefully planned detective work crumbled around me. Images flood my mind. The cracks in the brick wall, the gun pointed at my face. Sometimes I wish I could turn off my photographic memory.

Jonah looks back at me with concern. He opens his mouth to say something but is cut off by a screeching crackle coming from Julia's backpack. She stops and unzips her bag, pulling out what looks like a black walkie-talkie.

"It's a police scanner," she says, no doubt seeing our confused expressions. "I . . . borrowed it. From my father."

Jonah grins.

Holding the scanner to her ear, Julia listens intently. Excitement brightens her face. "It's another Plumas crime scene, in La Plaza Mayor." She gestures to a spot beyond the marketplace.

"Maybe it's the copy cat," Jonah says. "Maybe Ghostman left another clue!"

We turn to sprint for the plaza but are immediately forced to walk. Even though it's early morning, there are plenty of tourists out. Vendors block our path every few feet, trying to sell us everything from fresh figs to shell necklaces to fried dough. All the jostling on my cast is irritating, but I guess anything's better than going down an alley.

The police are already at the plaza, draping yellow caution tape around a statue of a man on a horse. The entire monument is dripping with blood. It's hard to see over the crowd that has gathered. I can just make out the spray-painted word *Muerte* and a sprinkling of white feathers in the sticky red mess. The air smells disgusting, like rotten hamburger.

"I see an *N*!" Jonah has a vise grip on my good wrist. "It's an *N*! A blue *N*! The initials are MNAM! I knew it! He's going to strike the museum!"

Before I can respond, I spot one of the Plumas about ten feet away. The dark tattoos on his neck are hard to miss.

He sees me.

"*¡Oye, muchacho!*" he yells. I know that means "Hey, boy!" and I know that means me.

"Run!" I hiss to Jonah, glad he's attached to my arm so I can yank him through the crowd. I turn back to see that the Pluma with long hair has joined the first one, and they're headed right for us.

In a flash Julia's beside me, panic on her face. "This way," she gasps, grabbing my cast with iron fingers. She pulls us both into an alley, running at a full sprint.

Don't think, just run. I keep my eyes on the sunshine peeking in at the other end of the alleyway. Almost there, almost there . . .

The third Pluma, the bald one who wasn't in the plaza, steps into the light, blocking our way. Julia stops and we crash into her. The other two thugs come up behind us.

We're trapped.

I want to scream, *WHY DID WE GO DOWN AN ALLEY? BAD THINGS HAPPEN IN ALLEYS!* Instead I breathe hard and cling to Jonah's hand like a petrified two-year-old.

The three Plumas look exactly like the pictures I drew of them two days ago: muscular, tattooed, and angry.

With a few grunted words, they fan out to take a post in front of each one of us. The kid with the weird chin hair and the gold-capped tooth steps in front of me. Jonah gets the one with the shaved head, who's still wearing a backwards baseball cap, and Julia squares off with Mr. Tattoos, who appears to be the leader.

Julia hasn't stopped talking. She's actually yelling at them, her Spanish fast and furious with a lot of hand gestures and rolling *R*s. The leader yells back at her, equally heated. I understand about every tenth word:

Julia: *Habada cha ca prrrrra ca pa. Miguel ca pa chrrraba.*

Head Thug: *Chepo do pocoto chabada.*

Julia: *¡Sí!*

Head Thug: *¡No!*

LAS PLUMAS

Me (to self): *We are going to die.*

Jonah: Uh . . .

Julia: *¡Prraca da sí, que no!*

Head Thug: *¡No y cha pe cena de Plumas!*

This goes on and on. Our two guards, Beefy and Beefier, are a fortress of muscle. They stare at us with narrowed eyes, occasionally slapping their fists against their palms as if they're imagining crushing our bones. They make the bullies at my school look like field mice.

While I'm concocting a lame plan that involves throwing a brick and making a run for it, Jonah suddenly dips his hand into his pocket. With shaky fingers, he pulls out a tangle of key chains. Does he have Mace? Or a pocketknife? What the heck is he doing?

The kid guarding him gets all tense, as if Jonah's just pulled out a gun. He yells something at Jonah, who cringes and holds up Mr. Q as if to ward off evil spirits.

Seriously? *This* is his defense plan? After all his talk about army tactics and ninja skills, *this* is what he comes up with? Now the Plumas are ticked off and shouting angry Spanish while closing in on us until our backs are pressed against the rough brick wall of the alley. I bend my knees, readying myself to try the leg-sweep maneuver that Detective Bovano showed me back in New York.

The bald kid tilts his head, examining Jonah's trembling hand. *"¿Te gustan los Yanquis?"* he says. He points to the Yankees key chain Jonah bought last year at a Yankees-Mets game.

Jonah doesn't speak, just blinks and blinks at him, but I understand what he's saying, so I jump in. *"Sí,"* I reply in a high-pitched voice. "We love the Yankees! We're from . . . er . . . *Somos de New York. Nueva York.*"

Bald Thug twists his ball cap around. It's a Yankees hat. It's a miracle.

Jonah finally clues into what's going on. "You can have it," he says, pulling the Yankees trinket off the wad of chains. He hands it to the thug, who grins.

Behold the power of baseball: uniting enemies as friends. Or at least, as hopeful acquaintances.

It's strangely silent in the alley, and I realize Julia has ended her screaming match with Head Thug. She's actually smiling. "It's all settled," she announces to us. "The police received false information. There is no new leader of Las Plumas. They didn't hurt the

temple or steal the mask. And they know that someone is trying to frame them. They want to help with
our investigation."

Uh . . . *WHAT?!*

Head Thug shifts his attention to me and Jonah.
He has piercings in his nose, ears, and eyebrows.
Tattooed flames curl up his neck and down his bare
arms. It's hard not to stare.

"Yo soy Nacho," he says. He points to himself,
speaking slowly so we understand him. Then he gestures to the goatee guy. *"Él es Chepe."* Then he points
to the bald kid with the Yankees hat. *"Él es Moco."*

From deep inside the folds of my terrified brain, I
have a vague recollection that the word *moco* means
"booger." A nervous giggle twitters in my throat. I
cover it with a cough.

Jonah steps forward to introduce us. "El Frijol,"
he says, motioning to himself. "And El Rojito." He
points to me. I do *not* want to be called Little Red,
but now's hardly the time to protest.

The Plumas all nod, then Nacho shakes hands
with Jonah. He spins Jonah's fingers in a fancy twist,
followed by a slap of palms and a fist bump. Then he
does the same thing to me, and before you know it

all of us are slapping hands and doing fist bumps and smiling tentatively at each other.

They gesture for us to follow them out of the alley, jabbering on and on to Julia in Spanish. I catch the words *Miguel* and *Coca-Cola,* and it appears we're going to go have a chat about Julia's cousin while sipping a refreshing beverage.

More handshakes, some slaps on the back, and it dawns on me . . .

We just became honorary members of a Mexican street gang.

Chapter 14

NEST

DAY 12

"Ready?" Jonah whispers.

Absolutely not. "Yeah," I croak through dry lips.

I can't believe this is happening. We're standing outside J. Gúzman's apartment, waiting for the signal from Julia. Turns out Ghostman's last name is Gúzman. Ghostman . . . Gúzman. Creepy coincidence, right?

I'll spare you the painful conversation we had with the Plumas yesterday. Julia had to do a ton of translating, and it took about four hours to hammer out a plan, but the important part is this: When Julia showed them a picture of Ghostman, the guy we think is framing them, they FREAKED OUT. They know who he is, see him come and go from his apartment all the time because Moco lives nearby. When they saw the picture, they wanted to go bust down his door and pound a confession out of him, but Julia suggested a subtler tactic.

So now we're here. Waiting for the signal. And then we'll break into Mr. J. Gúzman's apartment. Twenty-eight hours as Plumas and already we're turning to a life of crime.

The front door of the apartment building is wide open, no lock, no doorman. Ghostman lives on the first floor, which is perfect for a quick getaway. I look up the hallway, down the hallway. It's empty. Everyone's either at work or eating lunch.

We're in disguise, of course, wearing red and gold *Lucha Libre* masks like the Mexican pro wrestlers use. The masks cover our heads completely, with small holes for our eyes, nose, and mouth. It's hard to see, hard to breathe, especially under these stressful circumstances. The Mexican kids can totally pull off this look, but for some reason Jonah and I come off as scrawny, wannabe superheroes. El Frijol *y* El Rojito.

The walkie-talkie in Jonah's hand lets out a static squawk. "Nest to Frijol. Come in, Frijol," Julia says, her voice crackling over the receiver. She's stationed in front of the museum, monitoring all movement. The Plumas are in the museum alley, ready to cause a distraction if necessary.

"Frijol here, over," Jonah replies. Yesterday he magically produced a set of police-grade walkie-talkies from his suitcase. He refuses to tell me where he got them, and to be honest, I really don't want to know.

"Ghostman has entered the museum," Julia says. "You are clear."

We've been waiting all morning for Ghostman to leave his apartment. He finally did about twenty minutes ago, dressed once again as a museum guard. Who knows how long we have until he comes back.

"Over and out," Jonah replies. He clips the receiver onto his belt and pulls out a wad of surgical gloves from his pocket. I shudder to think where he got *those*. He snaps on a pair and hands me just one—I can't fit the latex over my cast hand. Then he whips out a pocketknife. "Cover me," he says.

Oh, wow, we're really doing it. I scan the quiet hallway while Jonah starts to rattle a knife in the keyhole. *Do this for Dad, you have to save Dad.* I wonder how you say *breaking and entering* in Spanish.

Rattle, rattle, rattle. Jonah began his lock-picking

career at age seven in his parents' dental office, where he unlocked every bolted door plus their safe. He's never looked back. Last spring I caught him researching how to hot-wire a car.

Sweat pools around my eyes, but I can't wipe it away because the mask is pulled tight against my glasses. And my cast is itching like crazy. Jonah shifts position and continues jiggling the knife in the keyhole. Someone's going to hear this. Any second now, Ghostman will come running.

Rattle, rattle, pop! The door swings open.

We freeze. No breathing, no movement. No sirens going off or police descending with machine guns. Just a dark hallway that leads into Ghostman's lair.

Jonah picks up the walkie-talkie and presses the on button. "We're in," he says. Then he clips it to his belt, shoulders his backpack, and takes a step into the darkness beyond.

I swallow hard and send up a quick prayer to both Chaac and Quetzalcoatl, promising that if we survive this, I will never, *ever* break the law again. Of course, two months ago I also promised I'd never lie to my parents or get involved in another police investigation.

Some promises are hard to keep.

Breathe . . . keep breathing. I inch forward as Jonah searches the dim hall with a flashlight. He flicks on a light switch. I close the door behind me. So far, so good.

We don't speak, just creep around, examining everything in our path. It's the smallest apartment I've ever seen. There's just one main room, big enough to fit a TV, a tiny couch, and a coffee table. There's a pile of blankets on the couch—I guess he sleeps there?—and an open duffel bag. Cautiously I peek inside and find four . . . no, five passports. Happy to be wearing a glove, I pick up each one, snapping photos in my mind: Joseph Brown from the United States. *Click.* Hans Bäcker from Germany. *Click.* Juan Gúzman from Mexico. *Click, click, click.* Five passports with five different names and nationalities. There's no time to process what it all means.

In the meantime Jonah is gently sifting through a stack of papers on the coffee table. Silently he motions me over. It would appear that Mr. Gúzman has been busy. Very busy. A set of museum blueprints are stretched out on the table, next to thick stacks of hundred-dollar bills and a plane ticket to Florida for two days from now.

Jonah's bright blue stare bores into me. I know what he's thinking: Ghostman is going to rob the museum and flee the country in the next two days.

A small white cardboard box lies empty and mangled beneath the table. Carefully I pick it up. The writing is in German and I have no idea what it says, but there's a picture of a fingerprint on the outside label. Some kind of fingerprint kit? Alarm bells clang in my head. *This is somehow linked to Dad's fingerprints!* I snap mental photos of the words so I can translate them later, then lower the box to its original spot.

Jonah steps toward a closed door, and I follow. It opens into an über-small kitchen. A kitchen that smells *awful*. Something is rotting, giving off a putrid, sharp stench that burns my eyes. My new panicked thought: Maybe Ghostman isn't just a thief. Maybe he's a serial killer who keeps body parts as souvenirs.

My pulse hammers in my ears, and my breath is hot and suffocating in the stupid mask. I flick a nervous glance over my shoulder, expecting to see Ghostman standing there with a hatchet, ready to hack us apart.

Jonah slinks forward. The smell seems to be coming from under the sink. He opens the cupboard slowly, slowly. Oh, no, it's a severed head. We're dead. Ghostman is a serial killer, and he's—

"He's Jewish," Jonah breathes.

Huh?

Jonah pulls out an empty glass jar from the trash. The inside is speckled with a horrid-smelling white film. "I'd know this smell anywhere," he says, forgetting the number one ninja rule, *Do not speak.* "It's gefilte fish. My grandpa chows this stuff. It's a Jewish snack." He studies the jar, then drops it back into the trash.

"What—?" I begin.

He holds up a hand and makes an irritated zipping motion across his mouth, as if *I'm* the only one breaking the No Speaking rule. I raise an eyebrow at him, though unfortunately he can't see it since it's hidden behind the mask, and back out of the fish-infested kitchen.

One more closed door to investigate and we're outta here. Thank goodness. I'm guessing the door leads to a bathroom, and I *really* don't want to search through Ghostman's toiletries, but I take a deep breath, turn the doorknob, and push.

I stop in my tracks. Up on a shelf above the sink sits the stolen mask.

The . . . stolen . . . mask.

It stares back at me, its face still cut in an angry grimace. What is it doing in here? Does Ghostman talk to it while he shaves in the morning or something? This is not okay on so many levels.

"Holy bleep!" Jonah whispers. He moves around me to get a better view. He reaches forward to gently lift the mask off the shelf. A warning chill shoots up my spine. Something's not right here.

"Wait!" I hiss, grabbing at his arm. "What if it's a booby—"

He pulls the mask down. It's connected to some kind of wire. A click echoes in the bathroom.

"—trap," I finish.

We wait in silence. Have we triggered an alarm or a camera or some kind of countdown to our ultimate doom?

Jonah's holding the mask like it's a bomb about to go off. Minutes tick by. Finally he releases a sigh of relief. "That was a close call," he whispers.

The walkie-talkie crackles to life. "Nest to Frijol, Nest to Frijol." Julia's voice is panicked, her words a jumble of shouts and garbled English and Spanish. *"Haba-cha-rrrápido-crackle-beep-Ghostma—Corre!"*

I grab the walkie-talkie from Jonah's belt while he

stands frozen in place, a stunned look on his face. "Nest, you're breaking up," I say. "Repeat."

"Prrrrrrcha-*beeeep-crackle-crackle*—hear me?" The walkie-talkie squawks and shrieks. It's impossible to understand. And then out of the whole mess of static and Spanish, one word comes through loud and clear:

"Run!"

Chapter 15

COUNTDOWN

It takes Ghostman twenty-three seconds to get back to his apartment. Twenty-three seconds! The museum is at least a four-minute walk from here. Who is this guy, Superman?

If we were in a movie, racing against a clock, it would look something like this:

- *THREE SECONDS: With strange calm, Jonah places the mask back on the shelf while Edmund has a heart attack behind him.*

- *TEN SECONDS: The boys sweep through the apartment, turning off lights, closing doors, making sure everything is in its proper place.*

- *SIXTEEN SECONDS: The apartment door is locked. A quick scramble down the hallway and out onto the front steps.*

- *EIGHTEEN SECONDS: Jonah pulls a soccer ball out of his bag and throws it to Edmund, who dribbles it between his feet with an Alarming Lack of Skill.*

- *TWENTY-THREE SECONDS: Mr. Juan Gúzman arrives at his apartment building, where two dumb kids are kicking a soccer ball down the street. He doesn't pay any attention to them.*

Once we're around the corner and out of sight, we rip off our masks and sprint to the alley behind the market where we first "met" Las Plumas. I've decided alleys aren't so bad when you've got the Feathers Gang on your side.

Julia and the others are already there, pacing in the narrow space.

"Ghostman has the mask! He has the mask in his apartment!" Jonah explodes into the alleyway like a hurricane. "And he's definitely going to rob the museum. We found blueprints!"

Julia's eyes grow bigger. Her mouth opens in shock. But Las Plumas are frowning, obviously not understanding Jonah's English.

"Uh," I begin. "The bad guy has . . . el mask-o." That can't possibly be right.

"*La máscara,*" Julia corrects me. She fires off a quick explanation to Las Plumas. They jolt at the news, and everyone starts speaking at once. Chepe even pulls out a pocketknife, like he's going to go for Ghostman's throat right here, right now. I know they're our allies, but I still edge closer to Jonah. Then Nacho holds up a tattooed hand and the alley falls silent.

He whips out a cell phone. "*La policía,*" he says.

He's calling the cops? I turn to Julia in panic. "What?"

"He'll leave an anonymous tip," she explains quietly as Nacho starts speaking to someone over the phone. "And I'll talk to my father."

"Oh." I guess she knows what she's doing. How she plans on telling her father about all this without revealing our little breaking and entering stunt, I have no idea. "We found a weird fingerprint box in the apartment," I say. "What if Ghostman is using it to frame my dad somehow?"

She gives me a reassuring pat on the back. "If the police search Ghostman's apartment, they'll find it.

They'll connect the pieces."

"*¡Qué no!*" Nacho's angry voice echoes in the space around us. He runs a hand through his dark hair, obviously frustrated with whomever he's talking to at the police station. Maybe the cops don't believe him because he's a kid. I know what that's like.

He hangs up and curls the phone in his hand like he wants to smash it against the brick wall. Lifting his piercing glare, he mutters something to Julia in Spanish.

She folds her arms and gives a curt nod in response.

"What's happening?" Jonah demands.

"The police think we are kids playing a joke," she says. "So now we . . . what's the expression?" She pauses, frowning as she struggles with vocabulary. "Now we take matters into our own hands."

Chapter 16

NOTHING BUT NET

SEVEN HOURS LATER

A single knock sounds on the door. I knock back twice, the signal that we're in position. One more "all clear" knock, then Operation Balloon Drop commences. A lame name but a solid plan.

My team is assembled behind me. Julia is here as translator and lookout, Moco is our muscle, and Jonah is the Loud Distraction in case we need to make a quick getaway. We're in the service alley behind the museum, waiting for Chepe to let us in through the back door. His brother is part of the catering crew that's hosting the opening tomorrow night, so Chepe jumped in as an extra helper. As for Nacho, he's posted out on the street in case a certain bad guy tries to flee down the front steps.

"How do we know Ghostman's here?" Jonah asks.

"We don't," I say, although I'm convinced he is.

"He knows someone broke into his apartment. That changes everything. He'll need to rush the job, which will make him panicked and sloppy. It's perfect."

Julia nods in agreement with my assessment. All eyes are on me, everyone awaiting our next move. She told the Plumas that my dad's an FBI agent and I have special training in police tactics. They were impressed and let me take the lead. I've tried to think of everything I've observed from working with the NYPD. Exits are covered, hand signals established, weapons ready (not really but it sounds cool).

I turn to Moco. *"Tú vas primero,"* I say. He nods and moves into position to lead the way when the signal comes. I'm doing it! I'm speaking Spanish in complete sentences! Two more weeks of hanging out with Las Plumas and I'd be fluent for sure.

We wait and wait. Julia and Jonah start chitchatting behind me. "Why is it Aztec gold?" Jonah asks. He points to the museum poster on the brick wall, its edges curling in the heat. "Shouldn't the exhibit be Mayan gold? I thought we were on the Mayan Riviera."

Julia shrugs. "It's all a part of Mexico now. And the Mayans valued jade, not gold. That's what makes my family's mask so special. The gold in it is very rare."

She touches the picture of the gold coins advertised on the poster. "The Aztecs loved gold. They made beautiful things with it. Until the Spaniards stole it and melted it down."

I keep looking over my shoulder, convinced we're going to get busted. A history lesson during a mission? "We should have silence from now on," I whisper. "Hand signals only."

Julia nods. Jonah salutes me. We get back to standing there, twitching nervously.

Three knocks on the door. I knock back once. The door swings open with a loud creak. Without a word, Moco leads the way and the four of us jog down a dark hallway. We know where to go: Chepe drew us a map of the place an hour ago.

We head into the main exhibit room, the space barely lit with two soft floor lights. It feels weird to be in a museum with the lights off, as if *we're* the ones about to rob the place. Despite the dim light, the Aztec gold statues and mountains of jewelry gleam in huge display cases by the far wall. Tables and chairs are stacked in the corner. And silver and pink balloons rest in a net overhead.

As planned, we dive under a long table that Chepe set up, complete with an empty punch bowl and cups on top. Once we're settled in the cramped space, we peer out, lifting the white tablecloth that just touches the floor. I'm on the edge closest to the wall, Jonah beside me, then Moco and Julia.

Moco unloads the gear from his backpack. A long fishing net that smells like the ocean, a flashlight for Jonah, and a machete for me—Moco's dad is a fisherman and had just the supplies we needed. He hands me the machete hilt-first. Jonah's hand starts twitching like he wants to touch it, so I shift away, closer to where I'll have to cut the rope. The long blade is heavy in my grip. I'm not going to lie, it's the coolest thing I've ever held, even cooler than the Taser I fired last spring.

And now we wait. I glance at my watch: 7:42 p.m. We have a nine o'clock curfew. We told my parents we'd be at the town's Festival of Flowers with Julia. Ghostman better hurry up and get here.

Ten minutes pass. No one's around except for the caterers in the other room, their voices a low hum mingling with the occasional clank of dishes. The exhibit rests quietly in the soft light. I count eighteen gold masks. Eighteen! Not to mention the ornate gold statues, big and small. No wonder Ghostman wants to rob this place.

Twenty minutes. It's unpleasantly warm under the table here. Moco's fishing net is starting to smell bad, like rotting fish guts and seaweed. My butt's asleep, and Jonah's dripping sweat on my arm. His face is flushed and queasy. I know it's killing him to stay still with so many people smooshed around him. He takes out Mr. Q and starts rubbing the statue's stomach with his thumb. I wonder if he's got the statue of Ah Puch hiding in his pocket. I hope not. There's something ominous about bringing the god of death on a stakeout.

Moco whispers something to Julia. She giggles.

"What?" Jonah says.

"He wants to know why you're holding Ek Chuah," she says. "The Mayan god of war. A troublemaker, not so good for our mission."

"Huh? This is Chaac, the rain god."

Moco says something else and points to the stick in Mr. Q's hand. Julia translates. "He says that it's the god of war because he's holding a spear." She shrugs. "I thought it was Ix Chel, the fertility goddess. The stomach looks . . . kind of pregnant."

Jonah clutches the key chain to his chest. "Mr. Q is *not* pregnant!" he hisses. "He's just chubby."

I lean over and shoot them an *Are you kidding*

me? We're on a mission! glare. They offer me sheepish smiles and get back to monitoring the exhibit.

It's almost eight thirty. We have to leave or we'll be late and my mom will have a coronary. Just when I'm about to call it off, a museum guard strolls in. I sit up, every nerve ending alive with adrenaline.

The guard comes to a stop in front of the treasure, tracing a finger over the glass by the pile of Aztec coins. He's in perfect position.

Jonah's leg is moving a mile a minute. Julia's squinting as if she's not quite sure what she's seeing. But *I'm* sure. We can only see his back and a slim part of his profile, but I know that dark hair, the side view of his mustache. It's Ghostman.

I hold up a finger.

Go.

Slinking out from beneath the table, I lift the machete and swing at the rope tied to the wall as hard as I can. The rope snaps and the balloons drop, a shower of pink and silver. Ghostman looks up, startled. He tries to scramble out of the way, but Moco's there, flinging the fishing net. It lands perfectly on Ghostman's head, making him trip and fall down. His body flails and flails, trapped beneath the web of rope. Just like we planned!

Julia and Jonah scramble out of our hiding spot. Moco is leaning over Ghostman, shouting at him in Spanish. Suddenly Moco rears back, shaking his head frantically at us—the signal to flee. What? Why?

"Mission aborted!" Jonah grabs me by the arm, yanking me away from my victory.

But this is our chance to catch Ghostman—why the heck are we leaving? We take off down the hallway toward the alley door, Julia leading the charge. One last panicked glance over my shoulder at the body thrashing under the net. This time I get a clear shot of his face: Dark eyes. Thin cheeks. Hair that's slicked back off his forehead.

Captain Ruiz.

Chapter 17

BENCHED

—————

DAY 13

Twenty lame hours later and it feels like the balloon disaster never happened. It feels like yesterday never happened.

After we fled the museum, we watched from a safe distance as Captain Ruiz stuffed Moco into a police car and hauled him away. Moco's probably rotting in jail right now and it's all my fault. My first real police operation with a team, and it ended in complete disaster. I can't believe Ruiz was dressed as a museum guard. Is he working undercover? Or working with Ghostman to rob the place? Julia told us last night that she'd talk to her father and call us right away.

She hasn't called.

It's five in the afternoon and we've called and texted her maybe a billion times today. No response; all calls go straight to voicemail. "We have to do something," Jonah says, his voice muffled against the pillow. "I think Julia's in trouble."

"You don't look so good," I say.

"I'm fine," he replies, but he doesn't pick up his head. He's wilted and pale on the mattress. No jumping on the bed, no dancing around with Mr. Q. He's the anti-Jonah, an imposter wearing ghost-white skin that's turning greener by the second.

This morning my father dragged us to Chichén Itzá, the Mayan city he's been researching for his book. Dad was right—it's an amazing place. It has a pyramid twice the size of Isla del Niño's, plus statues, buildings, and tall stone columns with cool names like Temple of a Thousand Warriors.

But my heart wasn't in the trip. I was worried and distracted the whole time: worried about Moco, worried about the evil Captain Ruiz, worried about my father being sent to prison. All because I'm the lamest undercover cop in the world.

Plan B is now in effect. At seven o'clock tonight, just two hours from now, we're supposed to return to the museum for the grand opening. Jonah and I will be with Julia and my parents, playing the role of dumb tourists. Julia will distract my parents with random Mexican culture factoids while Jonah and I canvas the area by the exhibit. Chepe will be a waiter with the catering crew, working the floor. Nacho will be staked out in the back alley, where we're sure Ghostman will try to escape. Moco was supposed to be covering the front door . . .

"Julia's in trouble," Jonah says, yet again. He fidgets with his new black leather bracelet, courtesy of Las Plumas. "What if her dad threw her in jail?"

I snort. "I seriously doubt it. They're probably just working it all out." We thought about grabbing a taxi to her house, but we were gone all day. Plus her dad might be home, and he's a really intimidating guy.

"Maybe Ruiz is working undercover and he's already arrested Ghostman," I add. Hey, there's an upbeat thought. The first of the day. Jonah looks so miserable that I decide to show him the comic strip I'm doodling to pass the time, the one of us in our Lucha Libre masks. "What do you think?" I say.

His answering smile is small and queasy, but it's there.

Voices in the hall snag my attention. My father's deep baritone, and another man's nasally voice. A nasally, mean voice.

Jonah sits up. The alarm on his face mirrors my own.

What the heck is Captain Ruiz doing here? Did he somehow find out that we were behind the balloon drop? Or that we broke into Ghostman's apartment? Has he come to take my father away?

We sprint to the door and yank it open, just in time to see Ruiz leaving my parents' room with his clomping *I hate everyone* swagger. He sees us in the doorway and smirks. "Enjoy your evening, *chicos.*" He slaps a small blue passport against his palm.

A passport?

Dad is standing in the hall, staring blankly at the retreating captain. I jog over to him in two quick strides. "What happened?" I say. "Dad?" He blinks at me with glazed eyes.

"I'm under house arrest," he replies in a flat tone. He rubs his forehead. "They took my passport. They found my fingerprints inside the mask's case. How . . . ?" The question dies in the air.

I knew it. I *knew* Ghostman framed my father. Last night I used my mom's computer to translate the German words on the fingerprint box I saw in his apartment, but it was only a stupid ad for some kind of skin lotion. Somehow Ghostman managed to put Dad's prints on the inside of the glass. A brilliant tactic to mislead the police. I'd almost be impressed if I weren't so angry.

Mom comes out of their hotel room, tears streaking her cheeks. My hands ball into fists. *Nobody* makes my mom cry. I'd like to kick Captain Ruiz. And demand he tell me why he was dressed as a museum guard.

Jonah nudges my elbow and I startle. He shows me the screen on his phone. It's a text, but I don't recognize the sender. Maybe Julia used a different phone?

EL HOTEL. 5 MIN.

Meet in five minutes. In the lobby, I guess? I nod to Jonah and clear my throat. "Dad, Julia wants to meet us in the lobby for a minute."

He nods. "All right." He looks at his watch, stroking my mom's back with his other hand. "Let's meet for dinner in twenty." Then he murmurs something to Mom and they head back inside their room.

We sprint for the elevators.

In the lobby, Jonah lies down on a long white bench by the front doors while I pace the floor in front of him. One-two-three, turn, one-two-three, turn. It's like we've switched bodies.

"We'll fix it," he says. "Tonight we'll catch Ghost-man in the act."

I don't respond, just pace and pace. How are we going to get my parents to the museum when Mom is a wreck and Dad is a zombie? How are we going to convince them to leave the hotel? Wait—I guess Dad can't leave the hotel. Is that what house arrest means? Pace, pace, pace. I have to help Dad, and to do that, I have to catch Ghostman.

I freeze midstep as the lobby doors slide open. In strides Nacho, the fearsome leader of Las Plumas. Even in a generic baseball cap and blue T-shirt, he looks like he might rob the place.

I run over to him, Jonah right behind me. *"¿Dónde está Julia?"* I say, for lack of a better opening. This conversation is going to be tricky.

Nacho shakes his head. *"Problemas."* He hands me a white envelope. *"Problemas grandes."*

"What kind of big problems?" Jonah blurts. "Uh . . . I mean . . . Where is she? *¿Dónde está?*"

Nacho frowns, the metal hoop in his mouth pulling at his lower lip. He points to the letter. "Julia." Then he holds up his phone. *"Si necesitas ayuda."*

Okay, the letter is from Julia. And Nacho wants us to call his cell if we need help. The text must have been from him. But why would we need his help? I thought we had a plan for tonight. An awesome catch-the-bad-guy plan.

Before I have a chance to ask what's going on, Nacho turns and leaves without another word. I glance at Jonah, who shrugs and motions impatiently to the letter. I tear the envelope open. It's a bit tricky with my wrist in a cast, but my teeth and healthy hand get the job done. Julia's handwriting is sloppy, as if she wrote in a hurry:

Jonah and Eddie,
    I am sorry I did not call today. My father took my phone. I told him everything. I had to. He is angry that we have been investigating. And very angry about the balloon drop.
    There is some good news: the police found birth records of Ghostman in Germany. You were right—he is the son of Pablo Valero, the famous bank robber! I heard my father talking about it on the phone. The police went to Ghostman's apartment, but it was empty. No mask, no passports, no blueprints. I told my father about the initials MNAM, and he believes it is a good lead. He and his men will be at the museum

tonight, setting a trap. They have posted
Ghostman's picture—the one you drew—at all
airports and train stations.

My dad won't tell me why Ruiz was dressed
as a guard. But he did let Moco go, calling it a
kid prank.

We cannot interfere with the investigation.
We must call off tonight's plan.

I am sorry,
Julia

The note shakes in my trembling hand. Ghostman cleaned out his apartment. He knows we're on
to him. Will he show up at the museum tonight? He's
probably long gone by now, vanished like . . . well, a
ghost. They won't catch him leaving the country. He's
far too clever.

With heavy steps, I walk over to the lobby bench
and slump onto the hard wooden seat.

"What does this even mean?" Jonah demands. He
plops down beside me and yanks the letter out of my
fingers. He stares and stares at it, as if expecting the
words to rearrange themselves into a better message.

I heave an angry sigh. Angry at the situation, not
at him. "It means we're done," I say.

He blinks at me, completely lost.

I wave my orange cast in the air for emphasis. "It means we've been benched for the World Series." I'm hoping the baseball metaphor will get through to him. Nothing, no response. "We're done," I repeat. "We're out. Kicked off our own case."

"But—" He opens his mouth, closes it, opens it again. I think he's going to come up with a brilliant plan, a plan that will get us into the museum wearing mustache disguises or ninja suits or whatever else he has stuffed away in his suitcase.

Instead he throws up on my shoe.

Chapter 18

LETTERS

TEN MINUTES LATER

Dinner is about as cheerful as a funeral. Dad is wearing his purple beret — to "lift our spirits," according to him — but it's as wilted as he is. He keeps making dumb jokes about how great it will be to be stuck at the hotel indefinitely because he loves the food and the beach and the warm weather. The joke falls flat, and I think my mom's on the verge of a nervous breakdown.

We're supposed to leave tomorrow. How can we leave without Dad? What will happen if he actually goes to jail?

During dessert, Mom's face crumples and she starts to cry. Dad wraps her in a hug, making shooshing noises against her hair.

"I'm sorry," I whisper, even though I know she can't hear me. I'm sorry she's upset and I'm sorry that

Dad is being framed for a crime he didn't commit, and most of all I'm sorry that Eddie Red has failed them.

"It will be all right, honey," Dad says in a low voice. "Let's go back to the room. We'll see if the lawyer emailed us those documents." She nods and they stand to leave, barely acknowledging us with a half-hearted wave.

"What now?" Jonah says. He's been quiet the whole meal. Quiet and pale.

I shake my head. No plan, no hope.

We get up and make our way across the dining room. Papi's standing by the buffet line, frowning at a tray of roast beef. He jabbers some instructions at one of the waiters, then spots us and waves us over. "You have my pictures, Rojito?" he asks with a huge, toothy grin.

"They're in my room," I say. "I can go get them now, if you want." I might as well do *something* useful with my time tonight.

He nods and rubs his mustache, eyeballing Jonah up and down. "What's wrong with you, Frijol? You sick? Montezuma take a bite out of you?" He chuckles, then points a finger in the air. "Lime and salt, that is the cure. I make you a glass."

Jonah lets out a weird whimper, as if the very thought of lime and salt will send him straight to the hospital.

Papi keeps rubbing his mustache, examining us both now. "I owe you a favor for the pictures. What do you need?"

I shrug. A miracle is what I need.

"I know!" he exclaims. "I make you my famous chocolate lava cake." He claps his hands as if it's decided. "Go relax by the pool. Enjoy your last night here. *Te veo en una hora.* I come find you in one hour, yes?"

"Okay," I say. I really don't want cake, but it's better than sitting in the room depressed.

After heading upstairs to tell my parents that we'll be by the pool, I grab my sketchpad and Papi's pictures from the bedside table and try to get Jonah to stay in the room and rest. He insists on coming down with me. Of course.

We ride the elevator in silence. I hate this. I hate being helpless, hate being kicked off my own case. I hate how upset Mom and Dad are. And most of all, I hate the feeling that's been scratching at the back of my neck ever since we broke into Ghostman's apartment, the feeling that we've got it all wrong, that we're missing a major clue. But we're not. The evidence is clear. The showdown is tonight at the museum. Case closed.

I glare at the elevator buttons. I hate them too, at the moment.

"Have you ever noticed how there's an *M* here for no good reason?" I gesture to the rows of elevator buttons: *LL, L, M, 1 . . .* "There's a lobby and a lower lobby, but there's no *M* floor. What is that, anyway? Mezzanine?" I press the *M* button, but it doesn't light up. "It's like the floor doesn't exist. Why do they even give us the option? It's a total waste of materials." I sound like a grumpy version of my father.

Jonah grunts in response. The side of the elevator seems to be the only thing holding him upright. For a bizarre moment I wonder if his new statue of Ah Puch is causing him these digestive problems. Ah Puch *is* called The Flatulent One, after all.

Out on the pool deck, dusk is falling fast. Everyone must be at dinner, because the space is completely quiet and deserted. We grab our usual beach chairs and turn them around so they're facing the ocean and the island beyond. The clouds are lit with pinks and oranges from the setting sun. One of the most beautiful views I've ever seen, if I weren't on the verge of completely freaking out.

The rumbling purr of Paco finds me, and I manage a small smile. I dig into my pockets and feed him some beef jerky I bought at the gift shop. Don't think I've gone over to the dark side of cat lovers. But he's just so cool.

After Paco settles by my feet with his treat, I sigh and pull out my art pad to doodle while we wait for Papi. I'm so unsettled. Ghostman . . . missing letters . . . stolen bank gold . . . I sketch and sketch, random thoughts flickering in and out of my brain. I might finally be losing my mind.

Looking down at the paper in my hands, I realize I've drawn a strange doodle of the supposed Hebrew letter that Jonah saw in the seaweed that first day on the boat. Wait a minute: according to Jonah, Ghostman eats gefilte fish, which means he might be Jewish!

"Jonah," I say. I flash him the picture of the sea-weed letter.

Jonah's eyes bulge out. I think he may throw up again—there's a patch of sand nearby he can use—but instead he whispers, "The aleph. I totally forgot." He sits up and grabs my pad. He better not barf on Papi's pictures.

"If Ghostman is Jewish, he probably knows some Hebrew, right?" I say. "What if he left the aleph there on the beach as a clue? Does it have special meaning? There has to be a reason. Everything's intentional with this guy."

Jonah scratches his head. "The aleph is the first letter in the Hebrew alphabet."

First . . . What does *first* mean in all of this? The Mayans were here first, so that's why he marked their temple? Bleh, not likely.

"Unless . . ." Jonah pauses and brings his eyes to mine. "The aleph can be a silent letter. It's there in the word but not pronounced."

I think of the stupid *M* elevator button. A letter that means nothing. Is that what the aleph is telling us? That the letter at the pyramid was meant to be passed over? Silent, invisible, meaningless . . .

Yanking the notepad from Jonah, I flip to a fresh

page. "Ghostman left letter clues at all the sites. We thought they stood for Museo Nacional de Arte Moderno." I draw the letters:

M N A M

"But if the letter at the Mayan temple is supposed to be silent, then you pass over it like you would an aleph," Jonah says.

I pause. The pounding waves on the beach are distracting me, the constant noise disrupting the images in my head. What was the letter at the Mayan temple? An *M*? I can only see fragments of the picture. The floor, one wall . . . what was the stupid letter? This has happened to me before, when sounds fracture the pictures in my mind. I hate it.

"It was the *A*," Jonah says quietly. If he knows I'm struggling, he doesn't comment. "The *A* is silent. It shouldn't be there." He leans over and draws the new group of letters:

M N M

"The *A*. Right." I try to tune out the roar of the surf, my mind practically smoking out my ears as I strain to think of where I've seen the letters *MNM* before. I stare out at the island. "There's a museum," I say, "at the bottom of that pyramid out there. Museo Maya del Niño. MMN. But they mostly had educational posters up. Nothing worth robbing."

Jonah leaps to his feet and starts pacing. "Ghostman is copying his father's crime from thirty years ago. He's distracting the police at the museum while he goes after the *real* treasure. We did it, we solved the case!" He lets out an excited whoop. Paco hisses beneath my chair.

The real treasure? Now I'm lost. "Is he going to rob a bank like his father did?" I say.

"No!" He points wildly to the island. "*El oro está con mi niño.* Niño means 'son' *and* 'boy' in Spanish. We've been looking for the wrong *niño*. It's not his son, it's his *boy,* as in Boy Island. The treasure is buried out there, in the tomb beneath the temple. *That's* why Ghostman smashed the temple floor. He was looking for the treasure site!"

Yes! This all makes perfect sense.

"It's a huge job," I add. "He needs to work without interruption, so he's distracting the police, sending them on a wild-goose chase to the museum in town."

Jonah smiles while he paces, his stomach troubles clearly forgotten. "We've done it," he keeps repeating. "We've done it. We figured it out!" He stops suddenly, gaping at the island with his mouth open in awe. No doubt visions of tombs and snakes and poisonous blow darts are dancing in his imagination.

"We need to get out there," he says. "We need a boat."

I agree completely, but how? There's a rather large stretch of ocean between us and the island, an ocean that I, for one, am not going to attempt to swim at night. In the dark. With a cast. And a sick Frijol.

And then it comes to me, the perfect solution. "We have a new mission," I announce. Julia may not be able to help us, but I have Nacho's cell number. And I have Papi. I stand up and grab my art supplies. "You go back to our room. We're going to need your spy gear. I'll meet you there in fifteen minutes."

"And what will you be doing?" he asks. His hand twitches wildly by his side.

I push my glasses up on my nose. "I'm getting us that favor from Papi," I say. "And we're going to need more than one."

Chapter 19

STEPS

TWENTY-ONE MINUTES LATER

"ROLP!"

I return to our room just in time to hear Jonah barfing again. Poor kid. How can he can go on the mission we have planned? But I know I won't be able to talk him out of it. Plus I really need him. I can't do this alone.

The conversation with Papi went as well as expected. I remembered Julia saying that he helps his brother sometimes in the marketplace, selling fried dough. So after I gave him the pictures of his daughters—which he loved—I asked him if Jonah and I could help out at the market tonight, part of a cultural learning experience. I also asked for his phone number in case my parents want to verify where we'll be. They won't call. They're way too distracted to check up on us. Papi didn't seem thrilled about any of it, and he made me swear on a jar of hot peppers that we—i.e., El Frijol—would be calm and quiet while we were helping out. I felt bad for asking so much of him, but what other choice do we have?

I knock on the bathroom door. "You okay?" I ask Jonah through the wood.

"I'll be right out," he shouts a little too loudly.

I walk over to my bed and find his old Darth Vader costume perfectly folded and waiting for me. It's a one-piece body suit with sticker decals on the front that are supposed to look like Darth's machine buttons. He wore it two Halloweens ago and it doesn't fit him anymore, but I'm shorter than he is and it will fit me just fine. Over my dead body am I going to wear this.

Jonah comes out, wiping his mouth. He's dressed in black sweatpants, a black turtleneck, and a black winter hat. The perfect outfit for nighttime spying.

"What's this?" I say, gesturing at the Darth suit.

"You know what it is," he replies. "You need to blend into the shadows. I told you to bring ninja gear on this trip and you didn't. This is the only backup I have. It will have to do." His face is a pale green. I never knew the human body could actually *be* this color.

His breath catches. He throws a hand over his mouth and sprints back to the bathroom.

"I'm not wearing this," I call after him.

"Of course — *rolp* — you are."

I sigh. Of course I am. He's right, I need to blend into the night, and all of my clothes are too bright. Why do I have to like the color red so much? Not to mention the neon orange cast on my arm.

Keeping my T-shirt and shorts on, I slide my legs into the black suit. What is this evil material? It feels like a horrible combination of plastic and nylon and old rubber that should come with a suffocation warning label.

Next are the arms. Carefully I pull the long sleeve over my cast. I glance in the mirror. Yep, I look like a complete tool. He better not have brought the mask. That's where I draw the line.

Jonah shuffles back into the bedroom. Now he has black ninja paint on his nose and across his cheeks, but there are still patches of pale green on his neck and forehead.

"You're really sick, huh?"

He holds up a hand. "I'm cool," he says in a tough-cop voice. "I missed out on the action in New York because of a sinus infection. It's not going to happen again because of stupid Montezuma and his stupid germs." As he speaks, he loads his backpack up with everything ninja: rope, carabiners, a pocketknife, two flashlights, a cell phone, and a camera. Not to mention Mr. Q. Then he pulls a small, white statue out of his pocket. A *new* statue.

"What god is that?" I say, dreading the answer.

He tosses the statue in the bag. "She's a goddess. Ix Chel, goddess of the moon, among other things. We need moonlight. Flashlights are for backup only." He pauses and looks up at me. "Papi?" he asks.

"Done."

"Parental units?"

"Done." I told my parents that we're meeting Papi at eight o'clock. I told Papi that we'd meet him at ten. We have a two-hour window to get to the island and catch the bad guy. This had better work.

"Boat?" he says.

"Taken care of." Obviously I couldn't ask Papi for a boat—he'd tell my parents for sure, being a responsible adult and all—so I called Nacho, praying he knew someone in the area who owns one. It was the shortest, strangest phone conversation I've ever had:

Nacho: *¿Qué?*

Me: *Hola.* It's Eddie. El Rojito. I need a boat. Uh
. . . *Yo necesito un barco.*

Nacho: *¡Un barco!*

Me: *Sí.*

Pause . . . pause . . . pause.

Nacho: *Veinte minutos.*

And that was that. "We're meeting Nacho in twenty minutes by the docks," I say. At least, that's what I'm hoping.

"Good." Jonah throws more stuff into the bag. A coil of metal wire, a tube of superglue, a . . . Slinky?

"How exactly are we going to capture Ghostman?" I ask, suddenly nervous.

"It'll be easy," he says, never slowing his movements. "We spray his eyes with Mace. Then you go for his knees, and I'll jump on his back. We have rope. And these." He holds up a pair of shiny handcuffs.

I rub my neck. It's dawning on me that maybe this is the worst idea we've ever had. "Should we call Julia, let her know where we're going?" *In case we run into trouble,* I mentally add.

He shakes his head hard. "No. Her dad has her cell phone. If we call, he'll tell your parents. You know he will." He pauses, scrutinizing me. He looks like a weird pale skunk in his face paint. "We'll call once we've captured Ghostman. We've got this, soldier. Let's roll."

I follow him down the hall. We slink into the emergency stairwell, run down four flights of stairs, and open a side door that leads to the pool complex. Total stealth ninjas. Except I'm in a Darth Vader costume, and Jonah's the color of charred pea soup.

Nighttime is coming fast, and a huge moon is rising above. I guess Ix Chel is doing her job. Sticking to the shadows, we wind our way around the patio and jump the short fence to get to the beach. It's dark enough that no one sees us. Not even Paco, which kind of bums me out. My nerves would be soothed by his loud purr at the moment. You know things are bad when you start missing a cat.

In the distance, I see a figure driving a small motorboat, the engine rumbling against the sound of rolling waves. Nacho parks at the hotel dock and gestures to us with an impatient wave. I grin. I did it! I got us a boat without the help of a translator!

Step one of Mission Bad Idea: Complete.

We race down the dock and jump into the rusty

boat. I slide onto a bench seat beside Nacho, and Jonah smooshes himself against me on the other side. Nacho's eyes go wide as he takes in our outfits. He shoves two life jackets at us without comment.

A *snap* of life jackets being buckled, the shift of a gear stick, and we're off.

"*¿La isla?*" Nacho says, pointing to the island.

I nod.

He gestures to the boat. "*Mi primo Juan,*" he says. He points to his watch, then makes a slicing motion across his neck. "*Diez minutos.*" I think I get it: his cousin Juan (go figure!) owns the boat and will kill Nacho if he doesn't bring it back in ten minutes.

I nod again and we continue without speaking. The only sounds are the water slapping at the boat, the sputtering grumble of the engine, and the occasional *rolp* coming from Jonah's direction. I clutch the seat for dear life and focus on the island ahead. Five minutes and we're there. Five more minutes, five more minutes.

We hit a pocket of really high waves. The nose of the boat dips down hard, then jerks up, bouncing us in our seats. Jonah's backpack flies overboard. "Mr. Q!" he screams.

We lost all of our gear, our cell phones, weapons, rope, and he's worried about a stupid statue . . . ? How are we going to call the police? Or capture Ghostman?

"Why didn't you tie it to something before we left?" I yell. "Like, I don't know . . . YOUR SHOULDERS?"

"Why do *I* have to be in charge of all the gear?" he shouts back. "Why didn't you bring any ninja stuff? You never—"

"*¡Chicos!*" Nacho's voice seems to boom everywhere around us. I flinch and squirm a little closer to Jonah. Slowly I turn my gaze to the pierced and angry Pluma. Except he's not angry. He's running a hand over his face, exasperated, as if dealing with pesky younger brothers. "*Estamos aquí,*" he mutters, gesturing with his head.

I look up in time to see the island's dock coming up on our left. With all my annoyance, I didn't realize how close we were to shore. Nacho kills the engine and wraps a rope around one of the posts. Then he pulls out a cell phone and flips it open. It's one of those older ones from a decade ago and is probably stolen goods. Not that I'm judging.

"*Mi número,*" he says, pointing to a number on the

screen. Then he flips the phone shut and slaps it into my palm.

Excellent. I slip it into my sock—there are no pockets on the Darth suit—and say *"Gracias"* with a grateful smile. I wish Nacho could come with us, but it's for the best he's leaving. If he's here when we call the police, they'll probably arrest him on sight for all the vandalism he and his buddies have committed.

With hurried fingers, Jonah and I unsnap our life jackets. Nacho stands so we can slide past him to climb out of the boat. Once we're safely on the dock, Nacho gives us a *Go get 'em* nod of encouragement. The boat rumbles to life, and he's gone.

We did it. We're on the island, ready to capture Ghostman!

Step two of Mission Bad Idea: Complete.

The sky is dark enough now to see the stars. It would be nice to have a flashlight, but I don't chew Jonah out about losing the backpack. Adrenaline and fear have replaced all annoyance. This is it. We're really going to do this.

Jonah gives me a thumbs-up and runs down the dock, heading for the forest that surrounds the pyramid. I follow, and we step into shallow tide pools, the water rushing up to our knees. Instantly the Vader suit suctions to my body. I shove through a small tangle of bushes. It's mangrove, which grows in clumps in the shallows. It takes a few steps for me to realize that sharp sticks the size of knives are tearing at my body. "Ow!" I whisper-hiss. The more I thrash, the worse it is. Something slimy brushes my hand. *It's just an iguana. Stay calm!*

I stumble out to a clearing, where Jonah's examining the jagged cuts on his arm. "Sorry," he whispers. "That must be our punishment for losing Chaac. Our blood sacrifice has fallen on sacred ground. Now he'll bring us good luck. I'm sure of it."

I'd like to point out that Chaac is currently resting at the bottom of the ocean and most likely Extremely Angry. Instead I sigh and rub the throbbing stings along my arms and legs. Time to get my head in the game.

We creep through the rest of the small patch of forest, over to the stone steps of the pyramid. I strain to hear . . . what? Ghostman digging away at the buried treasure? All I hear is the pounding surf and the hum of nighttime insects. I swear there's a distant rumble of thunder.

Jonah holds up his palm and flashes me a series of hand motions: he points forward, then makes a fist, then holds up two fingers, draws a circle in the air, then points again.

"Huh?" I say. We did *not* go over this back in the room.

He moves his mouth closer to my ear. I cringe at the thought of how much throw-up has been exiting his lips. "There are two sets of stairs," he whispers. "You take the front, I'll go around back. Time your footsteps with your watch. Take a step every two seconds. Starting at eight ten on the nose." He holds his digital watch next to mine to make sure they're still perfectly synced. "We'll arrive at the top at the same time. You go for his knees, I'll knock him out with a brick and tie him up with my shirt. Easy."

"No," I hiss. "We don't have any fighting skills, Jonah. Without our equipment, the tackling plan won't work." I bend down to fish a stick out of my sneaker. "We need to—" I look up. He's already taken off.

If I don't go, he'll be alone up there. I have no choice.

I jog into position and glance at my watch: 8:07. The warm breeze is turning cooler, rushing faster. Clouds move in above, covering the stars. Yep, Chaac is mad, all right. I wonder if Jonah's statue of Ah Puch fell in the water as well. Does the god of death get angry if you drop him into the ocean? And what about Ix Chel?

It's 8:09. The pyramid is a skyscraper rising above me. *You can do this. Think of Dad. You have to help Dad.* Maybe Ghostman won't even be there. Maybe we've got this all wrong and the cops will catch him over at the museum.

It will be 8:10 in three, two, one . . . I take a step. Pause. Step. Pause.

I climb while looking at my watch, a feat way too tricky for my coordination level. The stairs are über-steep and I'm crouched low, the Vader suit tightening around my legs. It will be a miracle if I don't wipe out. I wonder how Jonah's doing.

Step. Pause. Step. Pause.

Almost there . . . Four more steps . . . Three . . .

There's a shout. And a scream.

Jonah's scream.

Chapter 20

CROUCHING NINJAS, HIDDEN VOMIT

I sprint up the rest of the stairs, dash past the temple, and tear to the other side, where Jonah lies motionless on his back. Ghostman is standing over him with a flashlight, a shocked expression on his mustached face.

"What did you do to him?" I yell, finding a strong and angry voice I never knew I had.

Ghostman jumps in surprise and practically drops the flashlight. "Nothing," he says. "He startled me and I yelled and he lost his footing. Knocked himself out." He rubs a hand nervously through his hair. "Or maybe he fainted. I don't know."

"Jonah!" I say, kneeling beside him, pushing at his clothing to see where he's hurt. *Please be okay*, I think over and over again. *Please be okay*.

I run my hands over his chest, assessing his ABCs: airway, breathing, circulation. He's breathing fine. There's blood on his hands and all over his arms, but that's from the stupid bushes. Head injuries from falling? Gently I shift him, feeling the back of his head. No blood. He's getting a lump where he knocked himself out. He moans but doesn't wake up.

My fingers curl into the front of his shirt. I don't know whether to try to shake him awake or strangle him right here and now for leaving me alone with the Evil Mastermind Criminal. I go for option number three, which is to pretend to take his pulse while scouring my brain for some kind of ninja plan. Nothing's coming.

"You stupid kids," Ghostman splutters behind me. "What are you doing up here?" His English has no accent, as if he's lived in the States his whole life. I thought he was German. Or Mexican. Or both. Who is this guy? He shifts the flashlight around, training the light on me, then on Jonah, then back on me again. "I should report you. You are trespassing on private property. I am the curator of this temple." He motions to the stone walls behind him, then adds, "Where are your parents? Out on their fancy yacht, I'll bet."

Understanding strikes me like a lightning bolt from Chaac's ax. *He doesn't know who we are. He doesn't realize that we've come for him.*

I take a deep breath and launch into the skinny wimp act. Not a stretch.

"We just wanted to play a prank," I say, my voice cracking like I'm panicked and maybe about to cry. "Please don't tell my parents. We'll leave and we can just forget this ever happened." *Sell the act. Get Jonah, drag his body down the steps, and find the police station on the island, the one Julia told you about. The one that's probably abandoned right now since all cops are on the mainland at the museum.* I avert my eyes, pretending not to notice that Ghostman has two large duffel bags and there's a large hole behind him in the dirt of the temple floor.

He sighs. "Fine. Get your friend and get out of here. Wouldn't want you to miss Halloween." He gestures to my costume.

Costume mockery is fine with me if it helps with my *I'm just a dumb kid* act.

Time to get out of here. I shift my hands beneath Jonah's armpits, ready to lug him down the steps. This should be interesting with a broken wrist.

"Wait," Ghostman says. "Turn around."

I freeze. Do I obey? Or make a run for it? I can't leave Jonah and I can't carry him down the stairs at a sprint. I turn my head toward the light of the lanterns that are resting on the ground, praying that the dark night on my face is enough to disguise me.

Ghostman's eyes narrow. "I know you. You and your friend broke into my apartment!"

"What?" Now it's my turn to gasp. "No, we didn't."

He stalks toward me, murder in his eyes. "There's a noise-triggered camera in my kitchen. I couldn't see your faces with those *lucha* masks on. But the voices . . . two American boys, discussing my trash. It was you!" He yanks up the sleeve of my Darth suit. "And your cast!" With an iron grip he drags me over to his work site while I curse both my orange cast and the gefilte fish conversation Jonah and I had in Ghostman's kitchen.

This is the part where we were supposed to tackle the bad guy, tie him up, and call the police.

Step three of Mission Bad Idea: Total Epic Fail.

He forces me to sit by one of the crumbling temple walls, then paces back and forth, firing questions at me. "Who are you? What are you doing here? Are you working with the police? WHO ARE YOU?" he yells.

I square my shoulders and straighten my spine. "I'm Eddie Red."

He pulls out a knife. My shoulders slump.

"And what," he says, moving the blade slowly back and forth in the space between us, "are you doing here, *Eddie Red?*" He sneers at my name. Gone is the man who was concerned with Jonah's well-being. This new guy is mean and cold and calculating. I'm pretty sure we're dealing with some multiple personality issues. One for every passport.

"You framed my father," I blurt. I decide to go with honesty and play the father card. "I'm sure you didn't mean to," I add quickly. "You lifted his fingerprints to send the police off on a search for the wrong man. But now they've taken his passport. Please. I don't care what you're doing here, I just want my dad to be free so we can go home."

He blinks and stares and blinks some more. The surprise on his face indicates that he's shocked I figured this all out. Then he shakes his head, muttering, "You don't know anything." He kneels by one of the duffel bags. The knife gets put away, *thank goodness,* and he lifts out a roll of gray duct tape.

You have *got* to be kidding me. NOT AGAIN!!

"Give me your arms," he demands. I want to tell

him that I already know the drill, that I was tied up with duct tape in an alley only two months ago, but my mouth won't open to form words. I give him my arms.

Around and around he winds the tape. How am I not prepared for this after what happened in New York? He cuts the tape with a pocketknife. I can still run — I'll just have to kick Jonah down the stairs as I go. Ghostman pulls out more tape and goes to work wrapping it around my ankles. So much for running. He discovers Nacho's phone in my sock and tosses it over the side of the pyramid. Terrific.

Thunder rumbles and a heavy *splat, splat* of rain starts up on the stones as wind whips around us. I need time to think. I need to distract Ghostman. I need to get him monologuing.

"What should I call you?" I ask. "Joe Brown? Hans Bäcker? Or is it Juan Gúzman?"

He ignores me and puts the duct tape away.

"Your father buried the stolen bank gold here, didn't he?"

Still no answer. With his face devoid of emotion, he fishes a gold brick out of the hole and places it gently in one of the duffel bags. I guess that answers *that* question.

I try again. "You look a lot like him," I say. "You could be his twin. Or his ghost."

No response.

"If he's your father, why don't you have his last name?" I'm taking a wild guess here. After all my clever spying, I still have no idea what his real name is.

But it punches the right button. "My father was a great man," he snaps. "Of *course* I have his name!"

He doesn't look at me as he speaks, just keeps yanking gold bricks out of the hole one by one and placing them in the bags. "The government killed him," he says. *Clink, clink* go the bars of gold. "They said it was a heart attack. All lies!"

His words come in angry bursts as he spills his story. His mother was the daughter of a German diplomat living in Mexico. She fell in love with his father, Pablo Valero, a local street thug. She moved back to Germany and Pablo was supposed to come get her, but he was caught robbing a bank and died. After Ghostman was born, his mother brought him to the States, where she died three years later.

So many nationalities, so many identities. He truly is a ghost man.

"I figured out the *niño* connection," he says proudly. "Everyone thought he left it for his son. But he didn't even know I existed. So now I've come to take what's rightfully mine." He pats the half-filled bag of gold, then turns and gets back to work.

I wriggle my arms to try to loosen the tape. Pain shoots through my wrist. That's it . . . my broken wrist! The duct tape is wrapped around my cast. If I can just break the plaster off, I can free my hand, then free the rest of me. I can do this!

I wait until he turns away to dig for more gold bricks. *Smack!* I hit the cast against a jagged stone and suck in an agonized breath. There are no words for how painful this is. I press on. *Smack!* It's awkward with my arms strapped together, but it's working. The plaster is cracking and starting to crumble. It's working!

Thunder booms; the rain drives in heavy bursts. The yellow light of the lanterns flickers around us. *Smack!* I squirm and twist my arm. The cast is loosening, and with it, the duct tape. Just two more smacks and I'll be able to break free. *Breathe through the pain, Edmund. Breathe.*

"Oh, no you don't." Ghostman stomps over and shoves me away from the temple wall. I shrink into myself, defeated. Apparently even in a thunderstorm,

I'm about as stealthy as an elephant in a hardware store.

"I don't have time for this," he mutters. He yanks me to my feet, then leans over and lifts something out of the bag. With the wind and rain it's hard to see until he gets up close. It's something silver and shiny. The knife again.

"You're cutting me free?" I say in a hopeful and squeaky tone.

He smiles. "No, Eddie Red. You've seen too much. Now, who should I kill first? You? Or your little friend?"

He lifts the knife just as a strong gust of wind sweeps in, knocking us both off balance. Ghostman trips on a bag behind him and stumbles, dropping the knife to catch his fall. The weapon clatters down the side of the pyramid.

Just when I'm about to launch my body at him as a kind of human torpedo, he straightens up and pulls another knife from his pocket. A larger, sharper knife. Wiping the rain from his face, he steps closer, weapon raised. I scrunch my eyes closed and whimper. What can I do? I can't throw myself at him, he's got an eight-inch blade in his hand!

There's movement behind me, a stirring against the stone. I whip my head around. A very pale Jonah is stumbling to his feet, his red hair wild in the whipping wind. He wobbles forward one step, then another, until he's beside me, his face set in determination. Standing up tall, he looks Ghostman right in the eye.

ROLP!

Chapter 21

ADIÓS

THE NEXT MORNING

Beep . . . beep . . .

The blood pressure machine sounds in Jonah's hospital room, the cuff automatically squeezing his arm every half hour to record his vitals. I'm in a chair next to his bed, my head resting on the mattress. It's been hard to sleep through the constant hospital noise, but I still managed to get about three hours.

"I still wish I hadn't fainted like that," Jonah mumbles. "I always miss the good stuff." He turns on the television with a remote control. His face isn't green anymore, although he's still a bit chalky.

I sit up and rub a hand over my face. "What are you talking about?" I say. "You saved the day. You saved *me*. You *were* the good stuff."

When Jonah threw up back on the pyramid, his

projectile vomit hit Ghostman square in the eyes. Totally gross and awesome. Ghostman stumbled backwards and fell down the steep flight of stairs. Minutes later the police showed up, thanks to an anonymous phone call—aka Nacho worried about us in the storm. Apparently Ghostman broke a bunch of ribs and an arm and got a bad concussion from falling down the stairs. Or so they told me once a translator showed up at the police station.

Jonah shifts in the bed and winces at the IV in his arm. "I guess so," he says. He was rushed here last night when he started throwing up in the jail cell (not my best hour). The doctors discovered that he was severely dehydrated, and he's been on an IV drip ever since. They said he'll be fine to leave in a few hours. Turns out he has iodine poisoning, and *not* the tourist stomach bug. The symptoms are similar, but he brought this on himself. I have no polite comment on the matter.

A knock sounds on the door behind us. *"Hola,"* Julia says in a soft voice. Jonah instantly sits up and grins. I stand to give her my chair but she waves me off, instead dragging a chair over from the corner. "You made the front page," she says as she opens a newspaper up and lays it on the bed. She's already been by once this morning with a box of cookies from Papi, who forgave us for lying to him. Nicest guy ever.

"We did?" Jonah sits up even farther.

She giggles. "Not really. But the police acknowledge they had help from 'outside sources.' That's you." She points to the words in the article, but I'm more interested in what the headline says: *Hans Bäcker Valero, el "niño" misterioso.*

"That's Ghostman's name?" I say. "Hans Bäcker Valero?"

She nods. "He confessed to everything, how he framed Las Plumas and how he moved your father's fingerprints to the inside of the glass case. My family got the mask back. My cousin Miguel was released from jail. And your father is free to leave the country."

We all beam at each other. A moment of contented silence fills the room. Victory.

"I'm glad," I say. I figured my dad was free and clear when the police returned his passport an hour ago, but it's a relief to hear the words. Maybe he'll stop touching glass cases from now on.

Speaking of Dad, he and Mom are seated just outside Jonah's room. I can see through the big glass window that Dad's staring off into space, his broad face changing expressions every few minutes, from relieved to angry to confused. And . . . impressed? He catches me looking at him and offers me a small smile. The tension in my shoulders loosens a degree. Maybe he won't kill me when we get back home. Maybe we'll even celebrate our amazing detective work.

Mom turns to say something to him, sees me watching, and scowls.

Maybe not.

Julia reaches into her bag. "Las Plumas wanted to come visit you, but there are a lot of police here, so they decided to stay away. They made you a present. It's in the alley where we first met them." She pulls out her phone to show us a photo of red letters spray-painted on a brick wall. The letters read ¡VIVA EL ROJITO! ¡VIVA EL FRIJOL!

Jonah grabs her hand, and at first I think he's getting all romantic—in which case, I will flee the room—but then I realize he's examining the skin on her palm. Skin that's streaked with red paint.

"Did you help them?" he asks, awestruck.

She presses her lips together, fighting back a smile. "Maybe."

Another knock raps against the door. Jonah drops Julia's hand like it's made of poison. Her pistol-packing cop father is looming in the doorway. He says something to Julia in Spanish. Then he looks at me and Jonah, tips his hat to us, and leaves. I haven't seen Captain Ruiz at all, and I'm glad. Maybe he got fired for being mean to nerdy tourists. It feels good imagining it.

Julia's eyes are wide and sad. "Time for goodbye," she says. She hugs me, then leans over to kiss Jonah on the cheek. "I will miss you," she whispers to him. She stands and clears her throat. "I will visit you in New York next year, yes?"

Jonah is speechless, rubbing his cheek where she kissed him, so I jump in. "Of course," I say.

She smiles once more and waves goodbye.

Jonah sighs. He folds his arms, unfolds them, folds them again, bumping the IV tube with his movements. I nudge his arm with my elbow. "I'm going to miss her too," I say.

He sighs again. "She was the coolest girl ever. I

don't even have a picture of her. My stupid cell phone and camera are somewhere on the bottom of the stupid ocean."

"She has your email. She'll send you a picture."

He frowns. "I can't ask her to do that. Too creepy." He throws his hands up in the air. "It's like she never existed. My first girlfriend and I have no proof! No one will believe me back home."

Girlfriend? I shake my head. Then I lean over to grab my backpack from the floor. "I was going to wait and get it framed," I begin, pulling my sketchpad out. "But maybe now's a good time." I rip out a picture and hand it to him. A very nice, very pretty picture of Julia.

He blinks. And blinks. And grins. "It's über-awesome. I . . . I don't have a gift for you."

I wave him off. "You can make us T-shirts. Yours can say *I passed out in Mexico.*"

Still grinning, he places the picture on the table beside him. "And yours can say *Quetzalcoatl is my homeboy.*"

I smile and prop my arms on the bed, staring at the television. I can't understand the words, but people are screaming as a gross bloody skeleton chases

JULIA

them through a jungle. Some kind of treasure-hunter movie. I put my head down and close my eyes. A nap is a much better choice.

I guess Jonah agrees with me, because he turns off the TV and lowers the bed with the touch of a button. "I think we need a vacation," he says.

"Yeah," I reply. I couldn't agree more.

We leave the hospital three hours later and sleep the entire flight home. As I step out of the airplane and onto US soil, the hectic scramble of New York's JFK airport greets me with its loud noises and rude shouting travelers. I love this city.

We wait forever in line at customs. Dad bought some pottery bowls that must have questionable smells in them, because a patrol dog just went nuts when he sniffed at my parents' suitcase. So now Dad is being grilled by a policeman. The poor guy can't catch a break.

As I sling my backpack onto the table for a security guard to inspect it, a man up ahead catches my eye. I wouldn't think anything of him, but he keeps glancing over his shoulder like he's nervous. He's got white-blond hair, a goatee, and wire-rimmed glasses.

LARS

He stops just beyond the gates, staring at me with crazy, maniac blue eyes.

Fear freezes me. I know him. It's Lars Heinrich, the art thief who escaped in May. The art thief who isn't supposed to know I exist.

He watches me and watches me, his eyes fierce and probing. His shoulders stiffen; his mouth opens slightly in surprise.

Realization washes over me:

Lars Heinrich knows exactly who I am.

And *that* is a very, VERY big problem.

THE END?

JONAH'S TOP FIVE MAYAN GODS*

Soldier Jonah Schwartz here, reporting on the Mayan gods. And let me tell you, there are a *lot* of them! According to historians, there were more than 250 gods and goddesses worshipped across the Mayan empire. Some were more important than others. After a lot of research, I've come up with five who will make the perfect military team:

1. *Chaac (or Chak)*
The god of rain and lightning.
Assessment: He has a lightning ax. A lightning ax! How cool is that? His thunderstorm helped us battle the bad guy on top of the pyramid, so I'd say he's our number one ally.

*Based on skill during a mission and general level of über-awesomeness.

2. Ek-Chuah

The god of war AND chocolate.

ASSESSMENT: War and chocolate? A PER-FECT combination in my book. After a hard day fighting off bad guys, chocolate is all a hero needs.

3. Ah Puch
(*pronounced* Ah Pwash)

The god of death.

ASSESSMENT: Since Death is all-powerful, this is a no-brainer. He'd be a little creepy to hang out with since he's got loose skin and bulging eyes, but he's sometimes called The Flatulent One (The God of Farts!), so that makes up for his creepiness.

4. Ix Chel

The goddess of the moon, rainbows, earth, fertility, and medicine.

ASSESSMENT: I'm not suggesting we spray our enemies with rainbows, but she seems to control a lot of powerful things, plus we'll need someone with a solid medical back-ground when we're out in the field. You never know when one of us will get knocked unconscious or break a wrist.

5. Itzamná

The god of creation, the sun, writing, and healing.

ASSESSMENT: As the god of writing, he'll be great at sending out special military codes. And maybe he can shoot flaming balls of fire with his sun powers. Sometimes he can be invisible. Need I say more?

ACKNOWLEDGMENTS

It was such a journey (literally!) to write this second book. A huge thank-you to my agent, Kristin Nelson, and my editor, Ann Rider, who made Eddie and his adventures possible. Thanks to the talented Scott Magoon, Mary Magrisso, Colleen Fellingham, Candace Finn, Rachel Wasdyke, and the many other hard-working people of Houghton Mifflin Harcourt. Marcos Calo, as always, your illustrations are incredible!

Thanks to my readers: Ben Wells, Beth Charles, Drew Whitney, Rachal Aronson, Emily Miles Terry,

Jeanne Williams, and Autumn Williams. You guys rock!

Thank you to my friends and family for their love and support. Melissa Denecker: thanks for forcing me out of my writer's cave. To my husband, Ben, and my two wonderful kids: traveling to Mexico with you was the best trip EVER!

And to all the amazing people I've met in the Spanish-speaking world, my students, teachers, and friends . . . *Muchas gracias.*

EDDIE RED
UNDERCOVER 3
DOOM AT GRANT'S TOMB

Seventh grade is here at last. New friends, new classes, and a chance for Edmund to be a regular kid again. Everything is perfect . . . until a new grumpy teacher shows up at school: Mr. Frank— a.k.a. Detective Frank Bovano, NYPD. He's been assigned as Eddie's undercover bodyguard, but first he'll have to survive teaching chemistry class.

The elusive art thief Lars Heinrich is back in New York City, leading the cops on a wild-goose chase through the city's most beloved monuments. Is he searching for the lost crown jewels of Ireland? Or is his target Eddie Red, the boy who ruined his last robbery? When Edmund vanishes on a carnival ride gone wrong, it's up to Jonah, Bovano, and a Trojan horse to save the day. Will they rescue Eddie from the evil Lars before it's too late?

The clock is ticking.